NIGHT WITHOUT END

Men who live and work in the endless nights of the Polar ice-cap have to be tough. They have to know how to survive in conditions that would kill most of us in a few hours – temperatures many degrees below freezing, snow storms and ice blizzards, savage winds that blow for hours on end.

Peter Mason, Jackstraw, and Joss are experienced in these conditions. They understand the dangers of the cold, the winds, the storms. They understand and trust each other. A man's life often depends on his friends. But when a passenger airliner crashes on the ice-cap near their remote weather station, they soon realize that a new danger has entered their already dangerous world. There are four dead men on the plane, but two of them died from bullets, not from the crash. Soon a fifth man dies. The ten survivors seem like ordinary people. But are they? Who is doing the killing . . . and why?

OXFORD BOOKWORMS LIBRARY
Thriller & Adventure

Night Without End

Stage 6 (2500 headwords)

Series Editor: Jennifer Bassett
Founder Editor: Tricia Hedge
Activities Editors: Jennifer Bassett and Alison Baxter

To
Henry, Chantal and Robin

ALISTAIR MacLEAN

Night Without End

Retold by
Margaret Naudi

OXFORD UNIVERSITY PRESS

OXFORD
UNIVERSITY PRESS

Great Clarendon Street, Oxford OX2 6DP

Oxford University Press is a department of the University of Oxford.
It furthers the University's objective of excellence in research, scholarship,
and education by publishing worldwide in

Oxford New York

Auckland Cape Town Dar es Salaam Hong Kong Karachi
Kuala Lumpur Madrid Melbourne Mexico City Nairobi
New Delhi Shanghai Taipei Toronto

With offices in

Argentina Austria Brazil Chile Czech Republic France Greece
Guatemala Hungary Italy Japan Poland Portugal Singapore
South Korea Switzerland Thailand Turkey Ukraine Vietnam

OXFORD and OXFORD ENGLISH are registered trade marks of
Oxford University Press in the UK and in certain other countries

Original edition © Gilach, A.G. 1959
First published 1959 by William Collins Sons & Co Ltd
This simplified edition © Oxford University Press 2000

Database right Oxford University Press (maker)

First published in Oxford Bookworms 1992
This second edition published in the Oxford Bookworms Library 2000
7 9 10 8

ISBN-13: 978 0 19 423091 9
ISBN-10: 0 19 423091 0

Printed in Hong Kong

Illustrated by: Janek Matysiak

CONTENTS

I jumped through the window of the wrecked plane and landed on top of a dead man. Although it was completely dark inside the plane, I somehow knew that he was dead. I switched on my torch and saw that I was right. It was the second pilot, crushed between his seat and the plane's wreckage. Covering his horribly injured body with a blanket, I wondered how many other dead bodies I was going to have to deal with . . .

This sudden meeting with death was my first experience of human civilization in months. For four long months I had been working, with only a few other scientists for company, in a lonely scientific station on the Polar ice-cap in Greenland. The sudden sound of the plane which had broken into the icy stillness of that night had been our first reminder of the world we had left behind . . .

1

MONDAY MIDNIGHT

It was Jackstraw who had heard the sound first.

'Aeroplane,' he announced.

'Aeroplane?' I asked disbelievingly. 'You've been drinking whisky again!'

'Certainly not, Dr Mason,' Jackstraw smiled. We both knew that he never drank anything stronger than coffee. 'Come and listen.'

That was the last thing I felt like doing. I had been lying in my sleeping-bag for fifteen minutes and had only just succeeded in creating a little warmth inside it. My feet, which had been completely frozen, were beginning to come to life again and the idea of getting out into the sub-zero temperatures of our cabin filled me with horror.

'Can you still hear the plane?' I asked.

'Yes. It's getting louder and closer all the time.' I lay there, wondering what type of plane it could possibly be.

'Dr Mason!' His voice was urgent now. 'I think the plane's in trouble! It's coming lower and closer. It's a big plane – I can hear several engines.'

'Damn!' I said with extreme annoyance.

I got out of my sleeping bag and hurriedly put on several layers of clothes. They had already frozen up in the half-hour since I had taken them off. I went over to Joss, our radioman.

'Wake up, Joss. I think we're going to need you.'

The three of us climbed into our furs – trousers, jackets, hats, boots and gloves – and put on our snow masks, to protect our faces from the freezing cold outside. Then I went up the steps leading to the trap-door in the ceiling, our only exit from the cabin. I banged hard against the door to loosen the frozen ice which surrounded it.

Tonight the ice cracked easily, so we lost no time in getting out of the cabin. We gasped in pain as the bitter cold entered our lungs. The wind was even stronger than I had expected. Its sound, like that of a human being crying out in pain, was louder than usual, but above that sound we could now hear the roar of the plane's engines.

And then we saw it. It was less than two kilometres away, no more than two hundred and fifty metres above the ice-cap. I only saw it for five seconds but what I saw filled me with

2

amazement. It was not the small type of plane I was expecting. It was a huge passenger airliner. Terrifying visions flooded into my mind as I imagined the plane crashing, and the passengers being plunged into those freezing temperatures, sixty degrees below the temperature of the plane.

The plane had turned a full circle and was now slowing down. It seemed to be flying at a dangerously slow speed. Then I saw its landing lights come on.

'He's going to land!' I shouted to Jackstraw. 'He's looking for a place to land. Get the dogs. Tie them to the sledge. Hurry!'

I ran back to the cabin, trying to think of all the different things we might need in an emergency.

'Get all the warm clothes you can find, Joss,' I shouted. 'And bring sleeping-bags, blankets – whatever you can think of. Don't forget the fire-fighting equipment, and the snow sticks – and for God's sake don't forget the homing spool. We'll never find our way back to the cabin without that.'

Jackstraw was busy tying the dogs to the sledge with the help of Balto, the lead dog. Although the dogs were bad-tempered and unwilling, Balto showed his true qualities as a leader, growling and biting his team until they obeyed.

I hurried over to the snow-tractor and with great difficulty removed the frozen searchlight that we would no doubt be needing. Then we heard the roar of the plane's engines once again. This time they sounded very low and very near. The plane came into sight, passing within two hundred metres of us like a huge, horrible bird.

'He's coming down to the north of us,' I said.

'Good God, he'll kill himself,' shouted Joss. 'He'll crash into those small ice-hills.'

3

Our progress was slow and painful as we moved along, fighting against the bitter, icy wind. We were following the line of the radio antenna, that stretched eighty metres to the north and was supported at intervals by pairs of poles, four metres high.

Suddenly the roar of the engines became deafeningly louder. Throwing myself to the ground, I saw the plane fly directly over us. Then the engine noise suddenly stopped and I heard a

Suddenly the roar of the engines became deafeningly louder.

hissing sound, followed by another loud sound as the earth all around us shook, and then finally the sound of metal being torn apart. After that there was silence.

We had to act fast. Turning to Joss, I asked hurriedly, 'How long's the homing spool?'

'Four hundred metres.'

'We'll go east for four hundred metres and then turn north.' We set off immediately, making sure that we tied the end of the line from the spool to one of the antenna poles. Our lives now depended on that homing spool. Without it we would never find our way back to the antenna and then the cabin. It was our only guide in the darkness and the blinding wind, over iron-hard snow, where there were never any footprints to help us find our way.

We were running now. And as I ran, desperate thoughts flooded my mind. Were the passengers trapped inside the plane or had they been thrown out onto the ice-cap? If so, they would freeze to death within five minutes. How were we going to get them back to the cabin? And how were we going to feed them all if we got them back safely?

When we came to the end of our line, we turned north, now pushing snow sticks into the frozen ground every few metres to guide us on our way back. Then, quite unexpectedly, we came across it – a huge hollow that the plane had dug in the surface of the ice-cap. By some amazing piece of luck we had run straight into the place where the plane had crash-landed.

We ran on into the teeth of the wind and came in sight of the plane. It looked huge – huge and helpless. As I looked at it, I knew that this enormous, wounded bird would never move again.

2

I breathed an immediate sigh of relief on seeing that there was no sign of fire anywhere. Even the smallest flame would have been enough to cause total destruction if it had found the plane's petrol. We switched on the searchlight and saw that the tail and the main body of the plane were undamaged, but that one wing and the nose of the plane were very badly smashed. Then I caught sight of the two words 'British Airways' on the side of the plane. I looked at these two words in shocked amazement. What on earth was a British Airways passenger plane doing in the middle of the Polar ice-cap? I was certain that British Airways didn't fly any planes over this isolated part of the world. So how had this plane flown so far away from its normal route?

We ran carefully over the slippery ice, round to the front of the plane. There we saw the small ice-hill that had obviously caused the crash. The nose of the plane had taken the full force of the crash, and the control cabin and the windscreens were completely smashed. I dared not imagine what state the pilots would be in when we finally got to them.

Pointing the searchlight at the cabin, I tried to jump onto the lower part of the windscreen but I couldn't find anything to hold onto. Jackstraw, seeing me in difficulty, ran up and supported me from below. With my knees on his shoulders, I smashed away the rest of the broken glass in the windscreen.

In two minutes the hole was big enough to climb through.

I jumped down into the cabin and landed on top of a dead man – the second pilot. Never in my life had I seen such dreadful injuries on any man. I put my head out of the windscreen and shouted to Jackstraw, 'Bring a blanket. And the bag of medicines.'

Jackstraw needed no assistance in jumping into the plane. He was one of the strongest and healthiest men I had ever known. He jumped up, pulled himself through the windscreen and landed beside me.

I covered the dead man with a blanket and then turned to the chief pilot, who was still in his seat. He was unmarked but completely cold – colder than any living body could be, even in the Polar ice-cap. There was nothing I could do for him.

Not far away from him we found the radio operator. He was unconscious but still breathing, and he was bleeding heavily. Very gently, I slid my fingers behind his head and realized with horror that, even if he survived – which was unlikely – he would be blind for the rest of his life. The sight centre in his brain had been completely destroyed. I gave him an injection of a strong painkiller and covered him gently with a blanket.

Behind the radio compartment I found another dead body, the third officer, and then, in the small kitchen area, we found the stewardess. She was lying on her side and moaning softly. As she did not seem to be badly injured, we covered her with a blanket and moved on.

The passenger compartment was much warmer so I called out to Jackstraw, 'Carry the stewardess in here. She'll have a better chance of surviving.'

I then turned to the man who was standing nearest to the

7

door. Blood was falling from his forehead and he looked at me with a lifeless expression in his eyes.

'This might seem like a stupid question,' he said. 'But what happened?'

'You crashed,' I answered. 'Sit down for a moment. You'll be all right.'

To my surprise, there were only nine other passengers in the plane. Two men were lying between the seats near the front of the compartment. One was a big man with dark, curly hair, the other was smaller and older and was wearing a jacket that seemed far too big for him. To the left of them sat a man by himself. He was sitting straight up in his seat, looking anxious but fully conscious. He seemed unhurt and I noticed that he was wearing a priest's collar.

On the right side of the plane were two women and two men. One woman was elderly but very good-looking and her face seemed slightly familiar to me. The younger woman next to her was also expensively dressed, in a very fashionable dress and fur coat. Both women seemed completely dazed, as though they had been woken up from a long and very exhausting sleep.

The two men on the right were also more asleep than awake. One was a large man of about fifty-five, his thick white hair and moustache giving him the appearance of a typical army officer. The other man was thin, elderly, and very definitely Jewish. Both were unhurt.

So far, I thought with relief, only one of the passengers was injured – and he only had a cut forehead.

At the back of the plane, however, a girl of eighteen or nineteen was lying on the floor between two seats. As I put my hands under her arms to help her up, she screamed out in pain.

'Be careful!' she cried. 'My shoulder!'

A quick look showed that her left collar-bone was broken. 'Don't worry,' I said, trying to comfort her. 'I'll come back to you as soon as I can.'

In the last row of seats at the back I came across another man. From the unnatural position of his head I knew immediately that he was dead, so I turned and walked back up through the compartment towards the pilot's cabin. The whole situation was beginning to seem very odd. Why, for example, were none of the passengers wearing seatbelts? The pilot must have known that a crash was unavoidable at least fifteen minutes before the landing actually happened.

Jackstraw appeared through the door at the front of the plane. 'The stewardess refuses to come,' he announced. 'She won't leave the radio operator.'

'Is she all right?'

'Her back hurts, I think. She wouldn't say.'

The large man with the white hair and moustache suddenly came up to us. He was shaking with anger. 'What's happened?' he shouted. 'Why have we landed? What's the noise outside? And who in the name of heaven are you?' He looked like a man who might cause trouble, but, right then, I could understand both his amazement and his anger.

'You've crash-landed,' I said calmly. 'I haven't the faintest idea why. The noise outside is an ice-blizzard. As for us, we're scientists working on a scientific station about a kilometre away from here.'

I tried to push past him but he put out his arm. 'Just a minute, if you don't mind,' he said in a very serious voice. 'I think we need to be told a bit more.'

'Later,' I said sharply, pushing his arm away. 'There's a seriously injured man who has to have attention at once. We'll take him to safety and then come back for the rest of you.'

The white-haired man began to protest again, so I added, 'Just remember that if it weren't for us, you'd all be dead in a couple of hours, frozen stiff. Maybe you will be yet.'

The young, dark-haired man who had been lying on the floor smiled at me as I passed him. 'Can I be of any help?' he offered.

I accepted his help gratefully. We returned to the radio operator and found the stewardess looking at him anxiously. She was very pale and was shivering violently.

'I . . . I must go and see the passengers,' she said with some hesitation.

'It's a bit late to think about them, isn't it?' I responded sharply.

'I know. I'm sorry. I couldn't leave him.' She looked down at the young man at her feet and then said emotionally, 'Is . . . Is he going to die?'

'Probably,' I answered, and she turned away as though I had hit her across the face.

We lifted the radio operator onto the stretcher as carefully as we could, and tied him to it. Then the dark-haired young man and I lowered the stretcher down through the broken windscreen to Jackstraw and Joss, who were waiting underneath. After that we helped the stewardess down. I thought I heard her cry out in pain as she was being lowered, and remembered that Jackstraw had said something about her back being injured. But I had no time to worry about it now.

The dark-haired young man joined us on the sledge and we set out, with the dogs running as fast as they could – keen to get out of the cruel cold. The wind was behind us, and the frozen ground was as smooth as river ice. Balto, the lead dog, ran ahead, following without hesitation the route marked out by the snow sticks and the homing spool. In five minutes we were back in the cabin.

We lit the oil lamps and the stove, and tried to make the injured man as comfortable as possible. I told the stewardess to make some coffee, and left her and the dark-haired young man together. The three of us then left to return to the plane, taking with us the warm clothes we had lent them and some bandages.

The temperature inside the passenger cabin of the plane had dropped at least sixteen degrees and almost everyone was shivering, one or two of them beating their arms against their bodies to keep themselves warm.

I put the pile of clothes onto a seat. 'Share these out between you and be as quick as you can. I want you to get out of the plane at once. But perhaps one of you will stay behind to help me with this young lady,' I added, pointing to the girl in the back seat.

'Help you?' It was the young woman in the expensive fur coat who spoke. 'Why? What's the matter with her?'

'Her collar-bone's broken,' I said.

'Broken? But why didn't you tell us, you silly man?' the elderly lady said in concern.

'I forgot,' I replied. 'Now who—?'

She interrupted quickly. 'I'll stay behind. I'd love to help.'

Joss left the plane with the rest of the passengers and the two of us moved the girl to the front seat where we would have more space to work.

'Do you know what you're doing, young man?' the elderly lady asked me suspiciously.

'More or less. I'm a doctor.'

'Doctor, hey?' she said, looking at my smelly furs and my unshaven face. 'Are you sure?'

'Sure I'm sure,' I said in annoyance. 'What do you expect me to do? Bring out my medical degree from under my jacket?'

She looked amused at this, and patted my arm approvingly. While I worked, she talked to the young girl in a gentle voice and we learnt that the girl's name was Helene, that she was seventeen, and that she was from Munich, in Germany. I looked at the elderly woman as she spoke, knowing that her face was familiar but I couldn't think why. And then it came to me in a flash. She was Marie LeGarde, the famous actress. For more than fifty years she had entertained audiences all over the world, winning the hearts of all those who saw her with her warmth and generosity.

Her reaction, when I showed that I had recognized her, was one of surprise. 'But how did you know me?' she said.

'From your photograph, naturally. I saw one in a magazine only last week.'

When I had finished tying a bandage round Helene's arm and shoulders, Marie looked at me with approval. 'You do seem to possess some medical skills, after all, Doctor . . . er . . .'

'Mason. Peter Mason. Peter to my friends.'

Jackstraw and Joss returned with the sledge and fifteen minutes later we were back in the cabin. Joss and I helped the two women down the icy steps from the trap-door, but as soon as I was at the bottom I forgot all about them, and stared in disbelief at the picture in front of me. Joss, too, stared with growing anger and horror. The injured radio operator was lying where we had left him. The others were standing around him. To the left, at their feet, lay our RCA radio transmitter and receiver – our only way of contacting, or getting help from, the outside world. It was lying upside down, smashed beyond repair.

3

Half a minute passed in complete silence. When I did finally speak, it was almost in a whisper. 'And who's the fool responsible for this?'

The white-haired man who looked like an army officer stepped forward. 'How dare you, sir!' he exclaimed. 'We're not children to be—'

'Shut up!' I said quietly. He did not continue, and I looked at them all one by one. 'Well?'

'I'm afraid . . . I'm afraid I did it,' said the stewardess slowly. 'It's all my fault.'

'You!' I said in amazement. 'You're the one person who should know how important this radio is to us. I don't believe you.'

'I'm afraid you must,' said the man with the cut forehead. 'She was the only one near the radio at the time.'

As he spoke, I noticed that his hand was bleeding. 'And what happened to you?' I asked.

'I tried to catch the radio as it fell,' he explained.

'OK. I'll bandage you up in a minute,' I said, turning back to the stewardess and looking her straight in the eye. 'Well, perhaps you can explain how it happened.'

'I was just kneeling beside Jimmy here—'

'Who?'

'Jimmy Waterman – the radio operator. Then I got up. I

14

knocked the table as I was standing up and . . . the radio just fell off,' she said unconvincingly.

'Really?' I replied in disbelief. 'That heavy piece of equipment simply fell off the table?'

'It didn't just fall off. One of the table legs broke. That's why the radio fell off.'

I turned to Joss. 'Is that possible?'

'No.' His answer was short but left no room for doubt.

Once again there was an embarrassing silence in the cabin. Hanging up my furs and gloves, I turned to the man with the cut forehead and bleeding hand and started to wash his wounds. I was interrupted by the dark-haired young man who had helped me get the injured radio operator out of the plane.

'Look here,' he said aggressively. 'Don't you think you've been a bit hard on the young lady? After all, it's only a radio. We'll get you another one, I promise you, in less than a week, ten days at the most.'

As I looked at him, I saw that his earlier friendliness had now disappeared. His eyes were cool and intelligent, and he looked like a man who could deal with any situation, pleasant or unpleasant.

'There's one thing you don't seem to be aware of,' I said dryly. 'In ten days' time you may all be dead.'

The young man stared at me in disbelief. 'What are you talking about?' he said, his expression hardening.

'Simply this,' I said. 'That without that radio, which you think is so unimportant, our chances of survival are not at all good.'

As I spoke, a sudden thought hit me. 'Have any of you,' I said slowly, 'any idea where you are at this present moment?'

15

'Oh yes, I've told them,' said the stewardess quickly. 'The pilot must have flown beyond the landing field at Reykjavik because of the snowstorm. This is Langjökull, isn't it?' Seeing the expression on my face, she tried again. 'Or Hofsjökull? We were flying north-east from Gander and they're the only two snowfields or glaciers in Iceland in that direction—'

'Iceland?' I repeated, in pretended amazement. 'Did you say Iceland?'

She nodded dumbly, and everybody's eyes turned to me. 'My dear girl,' I said, 'you are, in fact, at a height of 2,600 metres and right in the middle of the Greenland ice-cap.'

Silence. The effect of my words was electric. It was as if each person's mind had stopped working at exactly the same moment. And then they all started talking at once. The stewardess came up and caught hold of my sleeve.

'It can't be! It can't be!' she said wildly. 'It just can't be Greenland! We were on the Reykjavik flight. We don't go anywhere near Greenland.'

The dark-haired young man put his arm round her shoulder, but she stepped back as though in pain.

I said to Joss calmly, 'Could you please tell our friends exactly where we are?'

His voice was clear and unemotional. 'In Greenland – about 1,200 kilometres from Reykjavik, 480 kilometres from the nearest town or village, and 640 kilometres north of the Arctic Circle.'

He spoke in such a calm, knowledgeable voice that there were no doubts left in anybody's mind as to where they now were. Then a wave of questions hit me. I put up my hands in protest.

'Please, ladies and gentlemen. I'll answer all your questions one at a time. I don't really know anything more than you yourselves except, perhaps, for one thing. But let's have some coffee and whisky now. I think we need it.'

The suggestion was eagerly welcomed, except by the man wearing the priest's collar, who seemed embarrassed at the offer of whisky.

'Go on, take it,' I said impatiently. 'It'll do you good.'

This was the only encouragement he needed, and he drank the coffee and whisky with noticeable eagerness.

While they were all drinking, I turned to the injured man, who was now breathing more steadily. The stewardess bent down near me. 'Is he any better?' she asked anxiously.

'He is a bit, I think, but still in a very serious condition. Let me have a look at your back. You seem to be in pain.'

'No, no. I'm all right,' she insisted.

'Don't be silly, my dear,' said Marie LeGarde, who had been following our conversation. 'He is a doctor, you know.'

'No!' she said fiercely.

I stopped insisting and turned to look at the whole group. What an odd-looking group they were! Dressed in their expensive suits, their hats and elegant dresses, they looked so strange against the bare, simple background of the cabin. Here we had none of the usual comforts of life – no armchairs, carpets, or curtains. It was just a box of a room, five metres by four, with eight beds on one side and our scientific equipment on the other. Tins of food, most of them empty, were piled up along the third wall. Ice was climbing up all four walls, reaching almost up to the ceiling in the corners. There were two exits from the cabin – one led to the trap-door in the ceiling, the other

17

to the snow and ice tunnel where we kept our food, petrol and scientific equipment. At the end of the tunnel was a very basic toilet system.

I looked up and down the bare cabin, then at this unhappy, shivering group of people, who had come straight from their luxurious Western world. What was I going to do with them all? They were most unexpected and unwelcome guests. I took a deep breath and spoke.

'Well, as you're going to be our guests, we might as well introduce ourselves,' I said. 'On your left is Joseph London, our radio operator.'

'Now unemployed,' added Joss, looking bitterly at the wrecked radio.

'On the right, Jackstraw. Look closely at him, ladies and gentlemen. If you all live to get home again, it will probably be thanks to him. He knows more than any other living man about how to survive on the Greenland ice-cap.

'As for me – I'm Mason, Peter Mason. I'm in charge of this scientific station. We don't usually live here alone. Five of our colleagues are away on an expedition inland. They should be back in three weeks' time . . . Well then, that's us. As for you, I know one person amongst you – Marie LeGarde.' Some of the group, who hadn't yet recognized the actress, turned and looked at her in surprise. 'But the rest of you will have to introduce yourselves.'

The man with the cut on his forehead was the first to speak. 'Corazzini. Nick Corazzini. I'm on my way to Scotland to take over a new tractor company.'

'You might be quite useful to us, Mr Corazzini,' I said. 'We've got an old tractor outside that's extremely difficult to start.'

Corazzini smiled, somewhat nervously. Then I looked at the man with the priest's collar.

'Smallwood,' he said. 'The Reverend Joseph Smallwood. I'm on my way to London for an important meeting of the Unitarian and Free Churches.'

'And you, sir?' I said, turning to the little man in the large jacket.

'Solly Levin. Of New York City. And this is my boy, Johnny,' he said, putting his hand on the shoulder of the dark-haired young man beside him.

'Your son?' I said.

'God forbid!' the young man was quick to reply. 'He's my manager, not my father. I'm a boxer, you see. Johnny Zagero's the name.'

'Yes, he'll be a world champion very soon,' added Levin proudly. He was keen to continue but I carried on quickly, turning to the young woman beside Zagero.

'I'm Mrs Dansby-Gregg,' she smiled. 'Perhaps you've heard of me?'

I pretended that I hadn't, although I had in fact seen her photo several times in the fashionable society pages of various newspapers. 'And this is my maid, Fleming,' she continued, pointing to the young girl with the broken collar-bone.

'Your personal maid?' I said in disbelief. 'And you didn't offer to help while I was bandaging her shoulder?'

'Miss LeGarde offered first,' she said coolly. 'Why should I?'

'Well, that leaves just the two of you,' I said, turning to the white-haired older man and the Jewish man.

'Theodore Mahler,' said the Jew softly. I waited, but he added nothing.

19

'Brewster,' announced the other. 'Senator Brewster.' The name was instantly familiar to me as he was a colourful character in American politics. 'I'm on a European tour to collect information for one of our political committees.'

I looked at the group again. What a crowd to be responsible for, I thought to myself, right in the middle of the Greenland ice-cap! A business man, an actress, a minister of religion, a boxer and his manager, a London society woman and her German maid, a Senator, a silent Jew and an emotional stewardess. And a seriously injured radio operator who might live or die. I had to get them all to safety, but how was I going to do it? They had no suitable clothing for the sub-zero temperatures, no experience of travelling in Arctic conditions. Most of them did not even have the strength to survive on this wild and cruel ice-cap.

My despairing thoughts were interrupted by a flood of questions from the group. How could the pilot have gone so far from the normal route? Had something happened to him? Was the plane's radio damaged? Why was there no warning of the crash?

I answered all the questions as best I could, insisting all the time that I knew no more than they did.

'But you said earlier that you did, perhaps, know one thing more than we did.' It was Corazzini who spoke. 'What was that one thing, Dr Mason?'

I decided not to mention my first thought, and quickly invented something else to say. 'Oh yes,' I replied. 'I remember now. I simply meant that we've recently noticed, in our scientific investigations, various disturbances in the atmosphere which can interfere with radio communication. This may

What a crowd to be responsible for, I thought to myself, right in the middle of the Greenland ice-cap!

21

possibly explain why the pilot got lost and came so far north.'

As I spoke, I could see the puzzled look on Joss's face. He knew, as well as I did, that what I was saying simply did not make scientific sense. The others, luckily, seemed quite happy with my explanation.

I returned to the injured radio operator and, with the help of the stewardess, bandaged his head as gently as I could.

'What do you think of his condition now, Dr Mason?' she asked.

'It's difficult to say. I'm not a specialist in brain injuries. If he were in a proper hospital, I'd say he had a good chance of surviving.' I looked at her anxious, exhausted face. 'Tell me, Miss . . . er . . .'

'Ross. Margaret Ross.'

'Tell me, Miss Ross. Why was the plane so empty?'

'It was an extra one,' she answered. 'We had booked too many passengers, so we had to put on an extra plane.'

'Well, at least, with only ten passengers you had time to put your feet up and have a short sleep.'

'That's unkind!' she said, looking deeply offended. 'I've never fallen asleep on duty before. And if it hadn't happened this time, I could have warned the passengers. I could have moved Colonel Harrison to a safer seat in the front and he might not have died. And Miss Fleming wouldn't have had her collar-bone broken.'

I looked at her, unsure of what to think. She was certainly behaving strangely, and I wasn't convinced by her anxiety about the passengers. I would have to watch this girl more carefully, I thought to myself.

Aloud I said, 'There's nothing to feel guilty about, Miss

Ross. The pilot probably had no idea what was happening until he was actually crashing.' To myself I thought, 'Either this girl really had no idea what was happening – or else she's an extremely good actress.'

We had a satisfying meal of soup, meat, potatoes and vegetables – all out of tins – and then we discussed the sleeping arrangements. Margaret Ross, the stewardess, said she wanted to sleep by the injured radio operator. That left the three women with a bed each, and the six men with five beds between them. Corazzini suggested they should throw a coin to see who should be the one to sleep on the floor. The rest agreed and Corazzini ended up losing, but he accepted defeat without any argument.

As soon as they were in their beds, I looked at Joss and moved towards the trap-door. Joss had no difficulty in understanding that I wanted to talk to him, so he followed me out of the cabin. The wind had died down a bit but it was colder than ever.

'I don't like this at all,' said Joss strongly. 'The whole thing is just too strange for words.'

'Amazingly strange,' I agreed. 'But how do we get to the bottom of it?'

'Earlier on you said you knew something that the others didn't. What was it?'

'Well, I think I know why none of them knew anything about the crash until after it had happened. They must have all been drugged.'

Joss looked at me. 'Are you sure?' he said softly.

'Absolutely,' I said. 'They all had that dazed look in their eyes, and their reactions were unusually slow. It must have been some kind of sleeping drug.'

'But I don't understand,' said Joss. 'Surely, on waking up, they would have realized that they had been drugged?'

'In normal circumstances, yes. But they were probably so confused that they must have blamed the crash for all their strange reactions.'

As we sat there shivering on the frozen snow, Joss thought out loud. 'It's simply not possible,' he insisted. 'How could anyone go around the plane dropping sleeping drugs into the passengers' drinks?'

'Just a minute, Joss,' I said. 'What happened to the radio in our cabin?'

'I've no idea. But the leg on that table couldn't just break like that. Someone must have pushed over the table deliberately.'

'And the only person near it at the time was Margaret Ross . . . Now tell me. Who in the plane is in the best position to drug the passengers' drinks?'

'Good God! Of course! It must have been her!'

I didn't want to waste any more time.

'Tell Jackstraw about our suspicions as soon as you get the opportunity,' I said. 'Now let's get back to the cabin before we freeze to death.'

Inside the cabin the temperature was forty-four degrees centigrade below zero. I lay down on the floor, pulled my fur jacket up over my ears to keep them from freezing, and was asleep within a minute.

4

MONDAY 6 A.M. TO 6 P.M.

When I woke up, feeling cold and very stiff, it was late – 9.30 in fact. Jackstraw was already up, and had lit the oil lamp. Outside, it was still as dark as midnight. At this time of year daylight was reduced to just two or three hours a day, at around noon. Ice now covered the walls right up to the ceiling. I could see from our scientific equipment that the temperature outside was now forty-eight degrees centigrade below zero.

Jackstraw looked fresh and fully rested, and was busily melting ice in a bucket on the stove. The others were awake too, shivering from head to toe, their faces blue and white with the cold. Marie LeGarde was the first to greet me and I immediately noticed that she was looking ten years older than she had looked the previous night. She had lost none of her concern for others, however. She asked the German girl how she was feeling and then, turning to Mrs Dansby-Gregg, enquired, 'And did you survive the night?'

'Survive is the right word,' was Mrs Dansby-Gregg's bitter response. Then, turning to the German girl, she said loudly, 'That coffee they're preparing over there smells delicious. Fleming, bring me a cup, will you?'

I took a cup and walked over to give it to the German girl. 'Have you forgotten that Helene has a broken collar-bone?' I said sharply.

It was obvious that she had not forgotten but this didn't stop her from saying, 'Oh, how stupid of me! I had completely forgotten!' Her eyes were cold and hard as she looked at me, and I knew I had an enemy.

Thirty seconds later I had forgotten all about it. I was just handing Marie LeGarde a cup of coffee when someone screamed. It wasn't particularly loud but it had a frightening quality in that bare, silent cabin. It was Margaret Ross, the stewardess. She was staring at the figure beside her, the young radio operator, and it was immediately obvious to me that he had been dead for several hours. I examined him. When I stood up, everyone's eyes were upon me. Zagero broke the silence.

'He's dead, isn't he, Dr Mason?'

'Yes. Internal bleeding in the brain, as far as I can tell.'

I lied to them. I was certain of the cause of death. Murder. The young man had been cruelly, cold-bloodedly murdered, as he lay unconscious, unable to move or help himself. Someone had covered his face with a pillow to stop him breathing, and killed him as easily and as quickly as if he had been a very young child.

We buried him out on the ice-cap. His grave was shallow. It was impossible to dig a deep one because the snow was too hard. The Reverend Smallwood said a few words over the grave, but he spoke in such a low voice and he was shivering so much that I couldn't catch anything he said.

Back in the cabin we had a small and silent breakfast and I noticed that Margaret Ross ate nothing at all. 'You murderess,' I thought to myself. 'Your performance as a sorrowful colleague is just not convincing, and soon the others are going to start wondering too . . .'

I had no doubt in my mind that she had killed him, as he lay unconscious. She had killed him, just as she had destroyed the radio and drugged the passengers. But why? She had probably killed the radio operator to stop him from talking. But why destroy the radio – the one piece of equipment so necessary for our survival? My head was full of questions that I couldn't answer. I looked at her again. 'She's either a very intelligent killer,' I thought to myself, 'planning her every move. Or else she's mad.' Neither possibility was a very comforting one.

Forcing myself to carry on as normal, I explained to the group, in detail, the reality of our situation. They sat listening, looking pale and sickly in the first greyness of the morning light.

When I finished, Corazzini spoke. 'So what you're saying, Dr Mason, is this. Your other colleagues left here three weeks ago in the modern snow-tractor and won't return for another three weeks. You've already finished most of your tinned food and have very little left. With thirteen of us here, we now have food for less than five days. That means a fortnight without food before they return.'

'Correct,' I answered.

'How long would it take to get to the coast in your old snow-tractor?'

'In good weather, perhaps a week. In bad weather the tractor just wouldn't complete the journey. It's too old.'

'Then why don't we wait for the other tractor to get back?' asked Zagero. 'We'll just have to stretch the food out.'

'Impossible,' I replied. 'We would all die – without a doubt. Humans can survive without food for a considerable time in normal weather conditions. But in these conditions we couldn't survive for more than two days after our food runs out.'

'What if we try and contact your colleagues?' Corazzini

suggested. 'I know this radio's broken but you said there was a radio on your old tractor.'

'It only works at a distance of 160 kilometres, perhaps 240, in perfect conditions. Our friends are more than 320 kilometres away and they won't be moving from their present position unless they really have to. They don't have much petrol to spare.'

'You have plenty of petrol here, I suppose?'

'Of course. There's about three and a half thousand litres out there,' I said, pointing to the tunnel.

'I see,' said Corazzini, looking thoughtful. 'Er . . . please don't think I'm asking too many questions – but I believe you contact your friends regularly by radio. Won't they worry if they don't hear from you?'

'No, not at all,' I replied. 'Hillcrest – he's the scientist in charge – never worries about anything. Anyway, their own radio isn't working properly at the moment. They'll probably blame it on that.'

'So what do we do?' Solly Levin asked anxiously. 'Starve to death or start walking? We'd better make a decision.'

'I've already decided,' I said. 'We leave tomorrow. All of us, that is, except Joss. He'll stay here to meet the others when they return.'

'Why don't we leave today?'

'Because we've got to get the tractor ready for the long journey. It'll take several hours. But first we'll go back to the plane to get everyone's luggage. You're all going to have to wear as many clothes as you can.'

I returned to the plane with Corazzini and Zagero, marking out a route with snow sticks so that we could find our way back to the cabin. The plane was cold and dark and it felt as though we were entering a grave. In the light of our torches we moved around like ghosts, only too aware of the dead bodies lying around.

Zagero was the first to speak in the deadly quiet. 'Are we . . . going to leave them here, Doc? Aren't we going to bury them?'

'Bury them? The ice-cap will bury them soon enough. In six months the plane will have completely disappeared under the snow.'

As I spoke, I saw Corazzini shaking a metal portable radio, with a sad expression on his face. He was listening to the noise coming from inside.

'Is it a total loss?' I said.

'I'm afraid so. And I only bought it two days ago – cost me two hundred dollars.'

'Take it with you,' I advised. 'Listen, there's Jackstraw now.'

We could hear the barking of the dogs and lost no time in loading the suitcases onto the sledge. There were so many that we had to make two trips to bring them all back to the cabin. When we returned, we were shaking with cold, and Corazzini's nose and cheeks were white with frostbite.

Lunch that day was soup and some dry cake – not what we needed to give us the necessary warmth and energy for the work ahead. Preparing the old tractor for our long journey was no easy job. While we worked, we had to put up a screen round the tractor to protect us from the knife-like wind. However, even with that protection and with two oil-lamps to give us some light and warmth, most of us had to return frequently to the cabin to beat some life back into our frozen bodies.

29

For long journeys the tractor could carry a wooden cabin that contained four beds. We had to put together all the separate pieces of this cabin, working in the freezing cold and near-darkness. It took us over an hour just to fix the floor pieces. Eventually, after several hours' work, the tractor was almost ready for the long journey ahead. By then we were all frozen to the bone, and our hands were cracked and bleeding.

We were just fixing the beds when I heard someone call me. It was Marie LeGarde. 'Would you come below for a minute, please? I want you to have a look at Margaret. Her back hurts – she's in quite a lot of pain.'

'I offered to see her last night. If she wants me, why doesn't she come and ask me?'

'Because she's frightened of you, that's why,' she said impatiently. 'Are you coming or not?'

I went back to the cabin, and having removed my gloves and washed my cracked and bleeding hands, I examined the stewardess's back. She had an ugly bruise under her left shoulder and in the middle of her back there was a deep cut which looked as though it had been caused by a heavy piece of sharp metal.

'How did you get this?' I said. 'And why didn't you show it to me yesterday?'

'I didn't want to bother you yesterday,' she said. 'And I've no idea how I got it.'

'Well, perhaps we can find out,' I said, looking her straight in the eye.

'Find out? What does it matter? Why do you seem so angry with me, Dr Mason? What have I done?' There were tears in her big brown eyes.

It was an admirable performance, I had to admit. I could have hit her, but it was admirable.

I lost no time. I pulled on my furs and snow mask and reached the plane in five or six minutes. I jumped up and climbed through the windscreen, then went straight to the small kitchen area where we had found the stewardess immediately after the crash. A thorough inspection showed that my suspicions had been right. There was nothing there which could have caused that serious injury to her back. I went through to the radio compartment and there found what I was looking for. The top left-hand corner of the radio cabinet was badly damaged and I also noticed a small dark stain and some threads of navy blue cloth on the corner. I looked inside the radio and saw that it had been deliberately and thoroughly wrecked.

Although my mind was working with painful slowness because of the freezing cold, I could now understand why the radio operator had sent out no alarm, no warning messages. He had had no choice. The stewardess must have been pointing a gun at him.

A gun! That thought, for some reason, made me think of the dead captain of the plane. I went over to him and lifted up his jacket. Sure enough, just as I was expecting, there was a bullet hole straight through the middle of his back.

With a dry mouth and my heart beating heavily, I walked through the plane to the passenger whom the stewardess had called Colonel Harrison. Carefully I lifted up his jacket. There it was, the same deadly little hole. I moved him forward gently and noticed that the seat behind his back was slightly torn. I noticed, too, that the Colonel had been carrying a gun. Without

31

hesitation, I took this and put it into my jacket pocket together with some bullets that I found in one of his pockets.

In his other pocket was a passport and wallet. The wallet's contents were disappointing – a couple of letters from his wife, some British and American money, and a newspaper article from a copy of the *New York Herald Tribune* just over two months previously.

For a moment I studied the article in the light of my torch. There was a small picture of a railway crash, and I realized that it was some sort of follow-up story about a train disaster in New Jersey, when a passenger train had fallen over the edge of a bridge and plunged into the water.

I was in no mood for reading, but feeling that this might be of some importance, I folded the article and put it in my pocket together with the gun and bullets. Just at that moment, I heard a sharp metallic sound coming from the front of the deserted plane.

5

For five, maybe ten seconds, I stood there without moving, as stiff as the dead man by my side. Only one thought, a terrifying and crazy thought, was racing through my frozen mind – that one of the dead pilots had risen from his seat and was walking towards me.

Then I heard the same sound again. It was the sound of someone moving about in the darkness among the wreckage. I hid behind a seat quickly. This time I was sure of one thing. The sound had not been caused by any dead pilot, but by a living person, the stewardess. It had to be her. She was the only one, apart from Marie LeGarde, who had seen me leave the cabin. She had already killed three times and she wouldn't hesitate to kill a fourth, now that her secret was no longer a secret. As long as I lived I knew, and she knew, that I was a danger to her.

Suddenly my fear was replaced by a wild anger. I pulled out the gun from my pocket and ran to the front of the plane. There was no one there, but I caught sight of a dark figure jumping out of the smashed windscreen.

I tried to shoot. Nothing happened. As I heard the sound of feet hitting the ground, I realized that I had not loaded the gun. Looking out of the window, I saw the figure hurrying round the left wing of the plane and disappearing into the snow.

Ten seconds later I was on the ground myself. It was now

snowing heavily but I could just see the figure running ahead of me, along the line of the snow sticks. Suddenly she turned off in a new direction. I turned after her, using her torchlight and the sound of her feet to guide me. Then I stopped and stood very still. Her torch had gone out and I could hear nothing at all. I cursed my stupidity. I should have gone straight back to the cabin. Instead I had been led out here, away from the snow sticks. Why? Not so that she could escape me. As long as we both lived, we both needed to get back to the cabin and we would meet there sooner or later.

As long as we both lived! I suddenly realized what a fool I had been. The only way she could really escape me was if I no longer lived. If I were shot here, no one would ever know. Probably at this very moment she was aiming her gun at me.

I switched on my torch and spun round in a circle, staring into the darkness and the driving snow. Nobody there, nothing to be seen at all. I moved quickly to the left and switched off my torch. I'd been foolish to switch it on at all. I had now let her know exactly where I was. Slowly and silently, I moved round in a wide circle, listening for the slightest sound. But I heard nothing, and saw nothing. It was as if I were alone on the ice-cap.

And then the dreadful truth hit me – I *was* alone. I was alone because shooting me would have been a stupid way of getting rid of me. The discovery next day of my dead body, full of bullet holes, would have caused a lot of awkward questions. There was a far more efficient way of getting rid of me. The most experienced man can get lost in a snowstorm on the ice-cap – and die of cold.

And I *was* lost. There was no doubt about it. But my anger, at being tricked, was so great that I was even more determined to survive.

The snow was now building up into a blizzard. I could see no further than a metre or two, and my torch was growing weaker. I decided that finding the plane, which was probably only about ninety metres away, would be far easier than trying to find the cabin. I turned into the wind, and within a few minutes I came to the deep impression in the snow which had been caused by the crash. Thirty seconds later I found the plane itself.

I walked round the wing, found a snow stick and started to follow the line. There were only five sticks altogether. After that nothing. Every one of them had been carefully removed. My chances of finding the cabin were now extremely small. Desperately, I removed the first of the five sticks and tried to place it in line with the end one. I repeated this with the next sticks, but in the driving snow and my failing torchlight, it was impossible to keep the direction accurate. I quickly abandoned this plan and decided to aim for the radio antenna. It was, I knew, about four hundred metres from the plane in a south-westerly direction.

With my back to the plane I walked steadily forwards, keeping the wind on my back and counting my steps. Just as I was giving up all hope, I bumped straight into one of the antenna poles. My joy was indescribable. I threw my arms round the pole and held it as if I would never let it go. Then my joy turned to anger as I realized how close I had been to death. I ran all the way back to the cabin, using the antenna line to guide me.

The first thing I noticed, on entering the cabin, was that the stewardess was wearing a fur jacket and rubbing her hands.

'Cold, Miss Ross?' I asked, trying to show concern but not succeeding very well.

'And why shouldn't she be, Dr Mason?' said Marie LeGarde, rising to her defence. 'She's spent the last fifteen minutes with the men on the tractor.'

'Doing what?' I asked.

'I was giving them coffee,' replied the stewardess. 'What's wrong with that?'

'Nothing.'

I nodded to Joss and he followed me into the food tunnel. I didn't waste any words. 'Somebody, out there, has just tried to murder me,' I said.

'Murder you!' Joss stared at me for a minute and then said thoughtfully, 'Well, I'm not really surprised . . . This crowd's capable of doing just about anything.'

'What do you mean?'

'Somebody has been looking through our explosives.'

'The explosives!' For a moment a picture of some madman trying to blow up our tractor flashed through my mind. 'What have they taken?'

'Nothing. That's the strange thing. The explosives are still all there but they're all over the place, mixed up with the fuse wires and our other equipment . . . Anyway, what happened to you? You'd better tell me.'

I told him, and I saw his face tighten. 'We've certainly got a cold-blooded and calculating killer amongst us!' he said softly. 'But we've got no proof, you know.'

'I'm going to get it,' I said. 'Right now.'

I walked back into the cabin and over to the stewardess. 'I need you to come back to the plane with me, Miss Ross,' I said coldly. 'There must be some food left on the plane and we're going to need every bit of food we can get.'

It took us only ten minutes to get to the plane. The snow was not so heavy now and we could see for several metres. When we arrived, I pointed up at the windscreen.

'You first, Miss Ross,' I said. 'Up you go.'

'But how can I?' she said helplessly, looking at the windscreen high above her.

'The way you did it before,' I said fiercely.

She tried to jump, but didn't get anywhere near the windscreen. She tried again, but still didn't manage it. On her third jump, I supported her from below, so that her hands could hold onto the windowsill. She pulled herself up a little way but then, crying out, she fell to the ground. Slowly and painfully she stood up and looked at me. What a wonderful actress she is, I thought to myself. What a clever performance!

'I can't do it,' she said shakily. 'I told you that I couldn't. What are you trying to do to me?' Then she turned. 'I'm going back to the cabin.'

'Oh no, you're not!' I shouted, catching her arm. 'You'll stay here where I can watch you.'

I jumped up and climbed through the windscreen, then reached down and pulled her up after me. Angrily, I led her to the kitchen area. 'A convenient place to drug all the passengers' drinks, isn't it, Miss Ross?'

'I . . . I don't understand.'

'Don't you? Then tell me this. Where's the piece of metal which caused your back injury when the plane crashed? Where is it?'

'I . . . I don't know,' she said. 'What does it matter? I don't understand anything any more.'

37

I pulled Margaret Ross to the front of the plane, where the dead captain was sitting.

I took her by the arm, led her to the radio compartment and shone the torch onto the top of the radio cabinet. 'Blood, Miss Ross,' I said. 'Blood from your back. And these navy blue threads are from your uniform. You were standing here when the plane crashed. It's a pity you fell. But at least you held onto the gun.'

Silence.

'You missed your line there, Miss Ross. You should have said "What gun?" Well, I'll tell you. The gun you were aiming at the radio operator. Pity you didn't kill him there and then. But you made a good job of it later when you used a pillow to stop him breathing.'

'Pillow?' Her brown eyes were wide with fear.

'Yes. Last night, in the cabin, you murdered that young man.'

'You're mad,' she whispered unsteadily. 'Quite mad.'

In answer I pulled her to the front of the plane where the dead captain was sitting. I pulled up his jacket to uncover the bullet hole in his back. 'I don't suppose you know anything about this, by any chance?'

As I spoke, she fainted and fell on the floor in a heap. Another fine performance, I thought for a second. But no, this was no performance. She had really fainted. Margaret Ross was completely unconscious.

It is hard for me to describe the feelings of guilt and self-hatred that I felt during those next few minutes. Looking at her as she lay on the floor, I wondered how I could possibly have been so stupid. Why hadn't I realized that with her back injury it was quite impossible for her to jump into the plane through the windscreen? Apart from that, she was not even tall or strong enough to manage the jump. I had been blind, blind with anger.

As she opened her eyes, I did my best to comfort her. 'It's all right, Miss Ross. I'm not really mad. Just an absolute fool. I'm sorry for everything I said. Can you forgive me?'

I don't think she heard a word I said. Only one thing was on her mind. 'Murdered!' she cried. 'He's been murdered! Who . . . who killed him?'

'I don't know. All I know is that you had nothing to do with it. And also, that the murderer killed not only once but three times – he killed the captain, and Colonel Harrison, and the radio operator.'

She shivered, this time out of fear, not because she was cold. 'I'm frightened, Dr Mason . . . I'm frightened,' was all she could say. I tried to stop her thinking about the killer, but she could think of nothing else. 'Why was I taken into the radio compartment before the crash?' she asked.

'Probably so that someone could point a gun at you and threaten to kill you if the radio operator didn't do as he was told,' I said.

'So who else was there?' she continued. Seeing the puzzled look on my face, she went on, 'Can't you see? If someone was pointing a gun at Jimmy, the radio operator, another person must have been pointing a gun at Captain Johnson. It couldn't have been the same person.'

Yet again I cursed my stupidity. Why hadn't I seen this before? It was obvious that there must have been two different people with two different guns on the plane. Good God, this was twice – no, ten times – as bad. Out of the nine people back at the cabin, two of them must be merciless killers who wouldn't hesitate to kill again if necessary. And I had absolutely no idea who they were.

I sat silently, lost in those terrible thoughts. 'I know what you're thinking,' she said. Her voice was unnaturally calm. 'At this moment you're suspicious of everybody, including me. Well, look at this.' She took off a ring from the third finger of her left hand. 'This is my engagement ring. Jimmy and I were going to get married at Christmas. Now do you trust me?'

For the first time in almost twenty-four hours I acted sensibly. I said nothing. I just sat and watched her as tears rolled silently down her face. When she buried her head in her hands, I reached out and pulled her towards me. She turned, pushed her face into the fur of my jacket and cried as if her heart was breaking. And I suppose it was.

I suppose too, that it was hardly the best moment for me to begin to fall in love with her. But I'm afraid that's how it was. Emotions don't wait for convenient appointments. They just happen. I hadn't thought about women since my wife had been killed in a car crash, four years ago, only three months after our marriage. Since then I had lived the loneliest of lives, working in isolated places, completely cut off from the company of women. And now, emotions that I had thought were long dead, were suddenly alive and kicking. As I looked down at the small dark head against my shoulder, I felt my heart turn over. I couldn't explain it, and didn't even try.

After a while the crying stopped. She murmured, 'I'm sorry,' and wiped her eyes with a glove. Then she said, 'What do we do now, Dr Mason? Now that we know that the crash was not an accident, and that the plane was forced down at gun point?'

'I wish I knew,' I sighed.

41

'But why did they kill Colonel Harrison?' she went on.

'Perhaps the drugs they put in his drink didn't work well enough. Perhaps he saw too much, or knew too much. Or both.'

'But now *you*'ve seen too much – and you know too much!' she said anxiously. 'Let's get out of here – please. I'm frightened!'

No sooner had she said those words than we heard a noise outside – a quiet knocking on the side of the plane. Reaching for my gun and torch, I jumped through the windscreen and landed flat on the snow. I waited, listening, but there was only the sound of the wind. Using my torch, I ran right round the plane but there was nothing to be seen, so I called softly to Margaret, who appeared at the windscreen. 'It's all right. We were imagining things. Come on down.'

'Why did you leave me up here?' Her voice shook with terror. 'Those dead men in here . . . It was horrible. Why did you leave me?'

'I'm sorry. I just didn't stop to think.' I put my arms round her, calmed her down and together we walked back to the cabin.

6

Jackstraw and the others had just finished the work on the
tractor when we arrived. At the first opportunity I went outside
with Jackstraw and told him everything that had happened.

'What are we going to do, Dr Mason?'

'We'll leave as soon as we've had some sleep.'

'For Uplavnik?' That was where our main scientific station
was, on the coast. 'Do you think we'll ever get there?'

I knew what he was thinking. Travelling in an old, unreliable
tractor with a group of people unused to arctic conditions was
bad enough, but travelling with two killers among us made the
chances of our ever reaching Uplavnik very unlikely. It was
obvious to the smallest intelligence that the killers, whoever
they were, would only avoid police investigation and
imprisonment if they were the only two people to come out of
the ice-cap alive.

'I just don't know,' I answered. 'But I know that we'll starve
to death if we stay here. I think we'll make one more attempt
to identify the killers before we leave . . .' I explained to him
what I intended to do and he agreed.

Returning to the cabin, I looked carefully at the nine
passengers one by one. It wasn't easy trying to decide which two
out of the nine were the killers. Dressed in several layers of
clothes, they all looked different, almost unreal. Each one of
them, at first glance, could have been a murderer or murderess.

But on a second glance, they were just a group of shivering, miserable, very ordinary people.

But were they so ordinary? I studied them one by one. Zagero – was he really a boxer? He had the physical strength of a boxer but he seemed too well-educated, and there were no cuts or marks on his face.

And what about his manager Solly Levin? He seemed to be everything that a boxing manager should be – he was almost too good to be true. And the same could be said for the Reverend Smallwood. He was mild, quiet, and rather nervous – a really typical minister of God. They were both so typical that I was suspicious.

Corazzini was a question mark. He was obviously a tough and intelligent businessman, but, unusually for a businessman, he had a physical toughness as well. Corazzini, in fact, was not typical, and I was equally suspicious of him.

And of the two remaining men, Theodore Mahler and Senator Brewster, I had my doubts about Mahler. But that, I had to admit, was only because he was thin and dark and had said absolutely nothing about himself during all our time together.

As for Senator Brewster, surely he must be innocent? But then a worrying thought came to me. How did I know that he was really Senator Brewster? Anyone could grow a moustache and pretend to be a middle-aged Senator.

My thoughts were becoming more and more confused. I thought about the women. The young girl, Helene, had said that she was from Munich. Perhaps she belonged to some political or criminal group? On the other hand, she was only seventeen.

Mrs Dansby-Gregg? She came from a world of high society that I knew nothing about. She was clearly a selfish and insensitive person, but she lacked the hardness, the toughness of a professional criminal. Or so I thought. But perhaps I was wrong.

The only one left was Marie LeGarde. Of her I had no doubts. She was above suspicion.

Gradually I became aware that everyone was staring at me. They had obviously noticed me studying them one by one. Still, I was glad to be the centre of attention because that allowed Jackstraw to enter the cabin, with his rifle in his hand, almost unnoticed.

With everyone's eyes still on me, I nodded in Jackstraw's direction and said, 'Yes. We always carry rifles on our expeditions, for use against wolves or other wild animals. Jackstraw is particularly accurate with a rifle, so don't try anything. Just raise your hands. All of you.'

While speaking, I pulled out the gun I had taken from Colonel Harrison. Senator Brewster was the first to react. Jumping to his feet, his face red with anger, he shouted, 'What ridiculous game do you think you're playing?'

Then he stopped, suddenly. A deafening crash from Jackstraw's rifle rang through the room. When the smoke cleared, we could see a hole in the wooden floor just where the Senator had been sitting. There was silence in the room as the Senator, visibly shocked, sat down again. There was now no doubt in anybody's mind that we meant business.

Zagero spoke next, his hands still up in the air. 'OK, Doc. We know you're serious. Can you explain what all this means?'

'It's simple,' I said. 'Two of you people are murderers.

45

Both have guns. I want those guns.'

'My dear man,' said Marie LeGarde slowly. 'Have you gone mad?'

'Not at all,' I answered calmly. 'If you want evidence, it's out there on the plane. The captain has a bullet through his back, one of the passengers has a bullet through his heart. And outside, buried in the ice-cap, you'll find Jimmy, the radio operator, who was murdered in his sleep. Yes – murdered. He didn't die because of his brain injury, as I said earlier on. He was killed, here in the cabin, with a pillow over his face. Do you believe me now, Miss LeGarde?'

She didn't reply. In fact nobody spoke. As they sat there in shocked silence, I studied their faces, looking for some sign of guilt, but I noticed nothing. Whoever the killers were, they were in perfect control of themselves.

'You will now stand up one at a time,' I said. 'Joss will search you for guns. When you are standing, be careful not to move. If you do move, you will be shot instantly.'

The first to be searched was Zagero, but nothing was found on him. The others were then thoroughly searched, one by one, but again no guns were found.

'We'll search your luggage next,' I announced.

At these words Corazzini spoke, softly and calmly. 'You're wasting your time, Dr Mason. Nobody would have left a gun in such an obvious place.'

'That may be so,' I answered. 'On the other hand I can't take any chances.'

'OK, then,' he was quick to say. 'Whose bag are you going to start with? That's my bag over there, and the brown one next to it is—' He stopped and stared up through the small window in the ceiling. 'Good God!' he cried out. 'What on earth's happening out there?'

'Don't try any tricks, Corazzini,' I said. 'Remember our guns.'

'To hell with your guns!' he said. 'Look for yourselves.'

He moved out of the way and I looked up through the window. Two seconds later I pushed my gun into Joss's hands and climbed out of the trap-door.

The plane was a blazing torch in the darkness of the night. A solid column of fire, clear and smokeless, was rising out of the central body of the plane. All around, the snow was blood-red, and I could hear clearly the fierce roar of the flames. Suddenly, the column of fire turned white, leapt up to two or three times its original height and then, a few seconds later, the petrol tanks exploded, with a thunderous roar across the frozen stillness of the ice-cap.

Almost at once the flames died down, and I didn't wait to see any more. I climbed quickly down into the cabin. 'Well, that's the end of the plane, it seems,' I said, staring round at the watching faces.

Corazzini was quick to speak. 'So you've lost your evidence, eh? The captain and Colonel Harrison, I mean.'

'No. The nose and the tail of the plane seem to be undamaged, for some reason . . . We'll forget the bags, Mr Corazzini. These criminals are professional. They wouldn't leave their guns in such an obvious place.'

'Well,' said Joss, 'the fire in the plane explains one thing, at least.'

'You mean the explosives? Yes, it certainly does,' I agreed. The explosives had been left untidy, I now realized, so that we wouldn't notice the missing fuse wire.

47

'What's this about explosives?' asked Senator Brewster. It was the first time he had spoken since Jackstraw had fired the gun near him.

'Somebody stole some fuse wire from our supply of explosives to set fire to the plane,' I explained. 'It could have been anyone – even you yourself. All I know is that the person responsible for the murders also destroyed the radio and stole the fuse wire.'

'And stole the sugar,' added Joss. 'Though heaven knows why they should want to steal some sugar.'

I happened to be looking at Theodore Mahler at that moment, and he gave a little nervous jump at the mention of the word sugar. I knew I hadn't imagined it. I looked away quickly, before he could see my face.

Joss went on. 'It was our last bag of sugar, a fourteen-kilo bag. I found a last handful of it lying on the floor of the tunnel, mixed up with other supplies.'

Supper was a most unpleasant meal. There was very little to eat – just soup, coffee and some dry cake. Nobody dared talk to anybody else. The same thought was on everyone's mind – that the person sitting next to them might be a murderer.

After supper I got up from my seat and, telling Joss and Jackstraw to follow me, I went towards the trap-door. Outside it had stopped snowing, and the wind had died down. In the clear night sky the moon was bright and more than half full.

'A traveller's moon,' I said.

'Yes,' Jackstraw agreed. 'The weather's perfect for travelling. We mustn't waste any time. We'll have to leave immediately.'

I turned to Joss. 'Will you be all right alone?'

'Yes. But can't I come too?'

48

'No, I'm sorry. Someone must stay behind.'

In the faint light of our torches we searched the tractor and sledges for guns. We examined every corner but found nothing. Disappointed, I returned to the cabin and announced our departure. 'Get your things together, and put on as many clothes as you possibly can. We're leaving now.'

It took us an hour, however, to get the tractor engine to start. But at last we said goodbye to Joss and left him standing by the cabin, a lonely figure in the moonlight. I wondered whether we would ever see each other again. He was almost certainly wondering the same thing.

Jackstraw, sitting beside me as I drove, looked as calm and determined as ever. His eyes were constantly studying the ice-cap as we moved along, looking for any signs or changes in the snow which could warn him of approaching danger.

Inside the wooden cabin on the back of the tractor the ten occupants sat shivering, and behind them came the tractor sledge with all our food, tents and equipment. Behind the sledge came the dog sledge with all the dogs, on long leads, running beside it – except for Balto, who always ran free, helping Jackstraw by warning him of any change in the snow.

The first thirty kilometres were easy. We had no difficulty with the route because we followed the big flags which we had put down on our last journey up from the coast. We found twenty-eight flags in all, but suddenly they came to an end – the rest had probably been blown away by the wind.

'This is where things get more difficult,' I said to Jackstraw. From now on we would have to use the compass to show us the right route. One of us would ride in the wooden dog sledge with the compass, fifty metres away from the tractor. The

We said goodbye to Joss and left him standing by the cabin, a lonely figure in the moonlight.

compass was quite useless in the tractor itself, of course, because of the effect of a large body of metal. When Jackstraw was on the sledge, I walked round to the tractor cabin and looked in at the ten miserable occupants, their faces white, their bodies constantly shivering.

'Sorry for the delay,' I said. 'I need one of you to sit beside me as a look-out. Perhaps you, Mr Mahler?' I said, looking towards him. He nodded silently and followed me to the driving cabin.

It wasn't difficult to get him talking. Once he started, he just seemed to go on and on. He told me that he was a Russian Jew who had been forced to escape from his country with his father. He had gone to America, had found a job in a clothing factory in New York, and later had worked for an oil company. Now that his wife was dead, he wanted to live in Israel as he had always dreamt of doing.

It was a sad story, of a life full of sorrow and hardship, and I didn't believe a word of it.

We stopped driving when the moon went down and I told our passengers, as they drank their black, sugarless coffee, that we would stop for just three hours. Beside me sat Theodore Mahler, looking uncomfortable and nervous. As soon as I finished my coffee, I whispered in his ear that I wanted to discuss something with him privately. He looked at me in surprise, then followed me out into the darkness.

I walked about a hundred metres away from the tractor, then stopped, switched on my torch and brought out my gun. I heard Mahler gasp and saw his eyes widen with fear.

'Don't bother to act, Mahler,' I said. 'All I want is your gun.'

7

Mahler raised his hands in the air. 'What gun? I . . . I don't understand. I haven't got a gun.'

'Turn round,' I said. I pushed the gun into his back and searched through all his layers of clothes, but I found nothing.

'Are you satisfied now, Dr Mason?'

'No. I'm going to see if there's a gun in your case. Anyway, I've got all the evidence I need.' As I said this, I shone my torch onto the handful of sugar that I had taken from his two pockets. 'Perhaps you'd like to explain where you got this from, Mr Mahler?'

'You know where I got it from,' was his answer. 'I stole it.'

'Yes. It's a pity that such a small mistake could lead to all your crimes being discovered. It was bad luck that I was looking at you when Joss mentioned that the sugar had been stolen. And it was bad luck, once again, that when we had our coffee just now, it was dark enough for me to taste the coffee in your cup – it was so sweet I couldn't even swallow it. By the way, what did you do with the rest of the sugar?'

'You're making a bad mistake, Dr Mason. I left the bag of sugar exactly as it was, except for the few handfuls I took.'

'Right. We're going back to the tractor,' I said. 'I want to search your bag, now.'

'No!' said Mahler forcefully. 'Look, Dr Mason, I don't want you to make a fool of yourself in front of the others. I think

you'd better look at this.' As he said this, he took a card out
of his pocket and handed it to me.

I stared at the card in shock and growing horror. I had seen
these cards many times during my daily work as a doctor. Once
again, my suspicions had led me in completely the wrong
direction. I folded the card, pulled down my snow mask,
stepped closer to Mahler and pulled down his mask as well.

'Breathe out,' I said.

I recognized it immediately – the sweet breath of the
advanced and untreated diabetic. As I gave him back his card,
I said quietly, 'How long have you been a diabetic, Mr Mahler?'

'Thirty years.'

I questioned him about his medical condition and didn't like
what I heard. The sugar he had stolen wouldn't help him for
long. Here was another dreadful anxiety to add to all the others.

'My apologies for waving a gun at you, Mr Mahler. But why
the hell didn't you tell me about your condition?'

'You had too many other problems to deal with,' he said
simply.

We walked back to the tractor and I announced to the group
that we would move off again in five minutes.

Mrs Dansby-Gregg was quick to protest. 'But you promised
us that we could rest for three hours.'

'Yes. But that was before I found out about Mr Mahler,' I
said.

I explained clearly and simply the facts about Mahler's
medical condition. 'Only two things can save Mr Mahler's life
now – special food or injections of insulin. We have neither. All
we can do, to try and save him, is to get him to the coast as soon
as possible, so that we can obtain one of these two things. That

means travelling at top speed, without stopping, until we get to the coast. Are there any objections?'

There were no objections in response to my aggressive question, and we started driving again. My anger at this new worry was deep and bitter. However hard we struggled to keep Mahler alive, sooner or later the killers would have to come out into the open. Then we would all die. The killers could not find their way to the coast by themselves, but when we were near enough, they would surely abandon us to die in the snow. Or shoot us all.

We gave Mahler extra food and hot drinks, made him stay in bed all the time, and kept him as warm as we could. I lit the stove inside the tractor and kept it alight while we were moving – a very dangerous thing to do. All this extra care embarrassed poor Mahler, and he tried to protest. The others, however, simply wouldn't listen to him, and showed the greatest possible concern for his health. It was almost as if Mahler's life had become, for each one of them, an important way of forgetting the misery, fear and suspicion that surrounded us all.

The weather was still good and we kept moving, with only very short stops. At the end of one stop Zagero called out to me from his seat at the back of the tractor cabin. 'There's something strange going on outside, Doc. Come and have a look.'

I looked out. A strange light was spreading over the sky, becoming stronger and deeper with every passing moment. Faint colours were beginning to appear, forming clear and very beautiful patterns.

'They're the Northern Lights,' I said. 'Is this the first time you've seen them, Mr Zagero?'

'Yes. They're amazing, aren't they?'

'Well, they're beautiful, all right, but they can cause trouble, you know. They make radio reception very difficult.'

'It doesn't matter if our reception's bad, does it?' Zagero remarked. 'The radio back in the cabin is smashed, and we can't contact your colleagues with the small radio in this tractor. They're too far away.'

'That's true,' I agreed. 'But we might be able to contact our main station in Uplavnik when we get nearer the coast.'

The moment I said this, I could have bitten my tongue off. I had given away my last remaining chance of calling for outside help. Radio contact was always difficult, but I might have been able to ask for help from Uplavnik before the killers showed themselves. And if Zagero were one of the killers, he would now try to smash our radio long before we got near Uplavnik.

I studied Zagero's face in the faint light. He was looking relaxed – but not too relaxed. On the other hand, if he had looked too calm, or too nervous, I would have been even more suspicious of him. Or would I? I was getting more and more confused. My previous suspicions had been so wildly inaccurate. But despite this, I had a growing feeling that Zagero was guilty. And almost certainly, I thought bitterly, my suspicion meant that he was innocent.

I turned to Margaret Ross and said that I wanted to speak to her outside. We sat down on the sledge and I asked her to try and remember the night of the crash.

'As I see it,' I said, 'there are three big questions to be answered. Why did the plane crash? How were the drugs put in the passengers' coffee? And how was the radio broken? If we can answer these questions, we might find out who the killers are.'

As we talked, I helped her to try and remember the events of that evening, one by one. She talked about how she had met her passengers, flown with them to Gander airport, flown out of Gander, and served the passengers their evening meal. Then she stopped and stared at me.

'Of course!' she said. 'Why didn't I think of that before? How stupid of me!'

She shivered, but went on talking, the words coming quickly as she remembered.

'There was a small fire in the men's toilet – nothing serious, just a few papers burning. I thought at the time somebody had been careless with a cigarette. Colonel Harrison discovered the fire, just after I had finished serving the meal – and before I served the coffee. Everybody got up from their seats and things were very confused for a few minutes. Anybody could have gone into the kitchen area then.'

She answered my next question before I asked it. Her big brown eyes stared into mine, and her voice was low, hesitant.

'Two people had asked me earlier at what time dinner would be served. Mrs Dansby-Gregg and . . . and . . . Mr Zagero.'

I bent forward in my excitement, nearly touching her face. 'Now, think back to that first night in our cabin, after the plane crash. Was Zagero anywhere near you when the radio fell onto the floor?'

'No, he wasn't.'

'But you turned round as soon as the radio fell. What did you see?'

'Mr Corazzini—'

'Yes, yes,' I said quickly. 'We all know that he tried to save the radio from falling onto the floor. But didn't you see anyone standing against the wall?'

'Yes, there was someone,' she said slowly.

'Who was it?' I said impatiently.

'Solly Levin.'

The short hours of daylight came and went, the cold deepened, and by the evening it felt as though we had been on that noisy tractor all our lives. We only stopped twice that day, at four p.m. and eight p.m. Twice I tried to contact Joss on the radio, but each time I was unsuccessful. I had promised him that I would try at regular intervals, just in case he had managed to repair the smashed radio since we had left. But we had both known that it was an impossible job.

Everyone was shaking and shivering in the cruel cold. From time to time somebody would jump down from the tractor and run alongside it, desperately trying to get warm. But we were all so exhausted from hunger, cold and lack of sleep that no one could run for more than a few minutes.

At ten minutes past midnight I finally gave the order to stop. We had been driving for twenty-seven hours.

8

Nobody slept that night, although we were all so exhausted. I think that if any of us had slept, we would probably have frozen to death. I have never known such cold. Even with twelve of us squashed inside that tiny space, even with the oil stove lit and lots of hot coffee inside us, we all suffered indescribably. How the elderly Marie LeGarde or the sick Mahler survived that night I still don't know.

At four o'clock I switched on the dim light and looked round at the circle of white and blue faces, now beginning to turn yellow with frostbite. It was a picture of total misery.

'Has anyone slept at all?' I asked. They shook their heads in silence.

'Is anyone likely to sleep?' They shook their heads again. 'OK. It's only four a.m. but if we're going to freeze to death, we might just as well freeze on the move.'

Jackstraw went out to try and start the tractor engine, and Corazzini and I followed, gasping and coughing as the cold air burnt through our throats and lungs. Inside the driving cabin I pulled out my torch and saw from our measuring instruments that it was −56 degrees centigrade, the lowest temperature I had ever experienced. Why should it happen now, I thought, when Jackstraw and I have as companions two murderers, a possibly dying man, and seven other passengers rapidly becoming weaker through exhaustion and lack of food?

It took us two and a quarter hours to get the engine started. Everything was frozen solid, and the engine had to be taken apart and heated up, bit by bit, on the oil stove in the tractor cabin. It was brutal, killing work; by the end the skin on our hands and faces was cracked and bleeding.

After an unsatisfactory breakfast of coffee and two tins of meat, shared out between the twelve of us, we continued our journey.

While Jackstraw drove, I examined Mahler. Although he was fully dressed, lying in a sleeping-bag and covered in blankets, his face was a blue-white colour and he was shaking uncontrollably with the cold.

'How do you feel, Mr Mahler?'

'No worse than anyone else, I'm sure.'

In fact he was already beginning to look thinner, but then so were all the others in the group, especially Marie LeGarde.

'Let me examine your feet,' I said to Mahler. They were deadly white, with no sign of life in them. I turned to Margaret Ross and asked her to keep two rubber bags, filled with hot water, constantly by his feet. Once again Mahler tried to protest, but I ignored him. I knew that frostbite in an untreated diabetic could mean that he would lose his legs.

At noon we stopped the tractor and Jackstraw and I tried, once again, to contact Joss. We were now nearly two hundred kilometres away from him. For ten minutes I sent out the call-sign on our radio and was just about to give up when Joss's voice came through the microphone.

'GFX calling GFK. GFX calling GFK. Receiving you faint but clear.'

I nearly dropped the microphone in my excitement. 'Dr

Mason here. Dr Mason here. Receiving you loud and clear. Is that you, Joss?'

'Yes, sir.'

Before I could say any more, he said, 'Captain Hillcrest is waiting to speak to you, sir.'

Jackstraw and I stared at each other, amazed. There was a warning in his eyes which I understood immediately. I said to Joss, 'Hold on. I'll call you back in two or three minutes.'

We picked up the radio and walked about two hundred metres away from the tractor, so that nobody could hear our conversation. Hillcrest's voice came over loud and clear. 'I'll try and keep this explanation short,' he said. 'On Monday afternoon we heard, on both British and American broadcasts, about the missing passenger plane. Yesterday we were contacted by Uplavnik. They say, although this is still unofficial, that the American and British governments are convinced that the plane hasn't been lost at sea but that it has landed somewhere in Greenland or Baffin Island. They've started a huge air-sea rescue search with many different countries sending ships and planes. Twelve US air force bomber planes have joined the search, Canadian ships are being sent out, and a British aircraft-carrier has already gone round Cape Farewell. All scientific stations in Greenland have been ordered to join the search – which is why we came straight back to the cabin to pick up petrol. What about you? Any important news?'

'No. Actually, yes. One of the passengers – Mahler – is an advanced diabetic. He's weakening rapidly. Contact Uplavnik by radio and tell them to get some insulin urgently.'

'OK. I suggest you return to meet us. We have plenty of petrol and plenty of food. With eight of us on guard instead of two, nothing could happen. We're only 130 kilometres behind you. We could be together in five or six hours.'

My first reaction was one of enormous relief, but this feeling didn't last long. Even before Jackstraw shook his head, I realized that returning to meet them would be the worst thing we could possibly do.

'Impossible,' I answered. 'The killers know that we've been in contact with you, so they'll be more desperate than ever. If we turn back, they'll have to act. I can't risk it. We must go on. Please follow us – as fast as you can. Explain to Uplavnik that it's essential for us to know more about this crashed plane. Tell them to find out the passenger list. Who, or what, on that plane is so damned important? We *must* know.'

Back in the tractor cabin the Senator was the first to speak – a sign, I suppose, that he didn't consider himself to be very much under suspicion. He was right about that.

'Have you made contact with your friends, Dr Mason?'

'Yes,' I replied. 'Joss finally managed to repair the radio in the cabin. He contacted Captain Hillcrest, who's in charge of the expedition group. And then, through some complicated radio engineering, he managed to get Hillcrest and myself in contact with one another. Hillcrest's now packing up and coming after us.'

'How long will it take?' asked the Senator.

'Well, he's at least 400 kilometres away and his tractor is no faster than ours.' Hillcrest's tractor was, in fact, three times as fast. 'It'll take him five or six days at least.'

The Senator nodded, and said no more. I wondered which of the ten passengers knew that I was lying. The person who had smashed the radio back in our cabin must have known that it could never be repaired again.

That afternoon, at about half past two, the temperature reached its lowest ever – a frightening 58 degrees below zero. Then strange things started to happen. The ice became so hard that the wheels of the tractor began to slip on flat surfaces. The dogs, although used to arctic temperatures, became so miserable that they cried and moaned in the freezing cold. As for us, whenever we went out of the tractor our breath immediately froze to ice, creating a thick white cloud around the head. Finally, as though all this were not enough, the tractor started to cause trouble. The radiator began to leak and to lose water with worrying speed.

Inside the tractor cabin things were not much better. The extreme cold was beginning to affect both the minds and bodies of all the passengers. They were losing interest in everything around them, wanting only to sleep and sleep through those long, endless hours. Later on would come the sleeplessness, the weakness, the inability to eat, and the nervousness that could lead to madness.

I looked at them one by one. The Senator sat without moving, looking more dead than alive. Mahler appeared to be sleeping. Mrs Dansby-Gregg and Helene lay close together in one another's arms, attempting to give each other some warmth and comfort. They were no longer employer and maid; hardship and misery had brought them together as human beings. Mrs Dansby-Gregg now showed a concern for Helene that I could not help admiring.

Marie LeGarde, lovable, brave, cheerful Marie LeGarde, was now a sick old woman, growing weaker every hour. There was nothing I could do for her. A day or two more of these conditions would surely kill her.

Solly Levin was so wrapped up in clothes and blankets that only one of his eyes was visible, but he still managed to look a picture of total misery. I had no sympathy to waste on him.

Margaret Ross was sleeping by the side of the stove, and I was now so fond of her that the sight of her pale, thin face caused me great pain.

Mr Smallwood was a great surprise to me. He seemed to have a hidden strength which helped him to overcome any pain or difficulty. He simply sat, looking relaxed and calm, and read his prayer books for hour after hour.

We stopped before eight that evening, because I wanted to contact Hillcrest again on the radio, but also because I wanted to give Hillcrest the chance to overtake us. I walked round to the tractor engine to empty the radiator so that the water in it wouldn't freeze while we were stopped. Over the sound of the liquid pouring out, I thought I heard someone behind me. I began to turn round, but I was too late. There was a white flash of light and pain as something heavy hit me on the forehead, and I fell, unconscious, onto the frozen surface of the ice-cap.

I could easily have died then, slipping from unconsciousness into a frozen sleep from which I would never have awakened. But gradually I heard Jackstraw's voice urging me back to life. 'Dr Mason! Dr Mason! Wake up, Dr Mason. Gently now. That's it.'

Slowly I tried to sit up. A flame of pain shot through my head. I tried to look around me but everything was unclear. For a terrible moment I thought that the sight centre in my brain had been damaged, but then I realized that it was only the blood from my cut forehead which had frozen on my right eyelid.

Gradually I heard Jackstraw's voice urging me back to life.

Jackstraw wasted no time with useless questions. 'Have you no idea who did it, Dr Mason?'

'No idea at all.'

'Any idea why?'

'None . . . Yes, I have. My gun . . .' I put my hand into my jacket pocket, but I was amazed to find that the gun was still there.

'Is nothing else missing?'

'Well, my bullets are here. Wait a moment – the newspaper article I took from Colonel Harrison's pocket. It's gone!'

'A newspaper article? What was in it, Dr Mason?'

'I never even read it. God, what a fool I am!'

Five minutes later I had washed and bandaged the cut on my forehead and we walked away from the tractor to contact Hillcrest on the radio.

'What news from Uplavnik?' I asked.

'Two things, Dr Mason,' said Hillcrest. 'The passenger list from British Airways in America has not yet arrived but newspaper reports give three names: Marie LeGarde, Senator Hoffman Brewster, and Mrs Phyllis Dansby-Gregg. The second piece of news is this. Our colleagues in Uplavnik think that some person on the plane must have been carrying something of the greatest importance – something where absolute secrecy is essential. Don't ask me what it was. I don't know. But it seems likely that the person who was carrying it was Colonel Harrison.'

I looked at Jackstraw and he at me. I felt close to despair. The man who had hit me on the head was much cleverer than me. He and his partner must have known that Joss couldn't possibly have repaired the radio transmitter in the cabin. They knew, therefore, that I must have been talking directly to

Hillcrest on his own radio, and that he must have been speaking from our cabin – or even nearer – since I had told them my radio only worked at a distance of about 200 kilometres. They knew that something important had made Hillcrest return from his expedition, because I had told them that he wasn't expected for another two or three weeks.

What proved their cleverness most clearly, however, was their guess that whoever knew the reason for the crash would be unwilling to tell me the details over the radio. They had therefore robbed me of the only clue that might have helped me discover what the details were, and possibly, who the killers were.

I spoke to Hillcrest again. 'Thank you. Please contact Uplavnik again and repeat that we urgently need to know the reasons for the crash. How far behind us are you now? We've only covered thirty-two kilometres since noon.'

'We've only done thirteen kilometres because—'

'Thirteen?' I shouted. 'Did you say thirteen?'

'You heard.' Hillcrest's voice was so angry it was almost unrecognizable. 'Do you remember the missing sugar? Well, it's been found. Your friends put the whole damn lot into the petrol. We can't move at all.'

9

We were on our way again just after nine o'clock that night.
At three in the morning we came to the Vindeby Nunataks –
a line of hills, 160 kilometres long. A narrow pass, with a well-
marked route, went through these hills, but it was a steep climb
up to the pass. The tractor wheels began to slip and spin on the
frozen snow and progress was slow and difficult.

We arrived at the entrance to the pass soon after seven. All
along one side of the pass there was a deep crevasse in the ice,
so deep that there seemed to be no bottom to it. I decided to
wait for the two or three brief hours of daylight before we
drove on.

At eight o'clock we contacted Hillcrest by radio. He had only
managed to advance a few kilometres in the previous twelve
hours. They had had to take apart and clean the engine, and
were now having to purify every litre of the sugared petrol –
a slow and difficult job. The other piece of depressing news was
that Uplavnik had no further information about the crash.

We started moving again after a three-hour stop. The steady
rise in temperature (it was now less than −34 degrees) had not
helped Marie LeGarde and Mahler, who were both very sick
people. They rode on the dog sledge while the others got out
of the tractor and walked. I did not want to risk an accident
with the tractor sliding into the crevasse.

We made good progress and by noon we were already more

than half-way through. Then, just as we had entered the narrowest and most dangerous part of the pass, Corazzini ran up to the tractor, waving at me to stop.

'There's trouble, Doc,' he said quickly. 'Someone's fallen over the edge. Come on. Quick.'

'Who?' I jumped out of the driver's seat, forgetting all about the gun I always kept beside the tractor door.

'The German girl. She slipped and fell. Your friend's gone after her.'

I looked over the edge of the crevasse and gasped. At the top the walls of the crevasse were no more than two metres apart. But lower down they curved away from each other and widened out to form a huge cave that disappeared into darkness. To the left, six metres below, the two walls were joined together by a snow and ice bridge about five metres long. Jackstraw was standing on this bridge, with his right arm around the dazed Helene. He must have jumped down onto the snow bridge to prevent her from falling off the edge of the bridge, where she had landed after her fall.

'Are you all right?' I shouted.

'I think my left arm's broken,' Jackstraw replied conversationally. 'Would you please hurry, Dr Mason? I think this bridge will break very soon.'

I had to think fast. Ropes? No. With Jackstraw's broken arm and Helene's broken collar-bone neither of them could tie a rope. Lower someone down into the crevasse on the end of a rope? But how would we take the weight on the slippery ice without being pulled over the edge ourselves?

I ran back to the tractor sledge and saw the answer at once – the four pieces of wood we always carried for emergency

68

bridges. They were four metres long and eight centimetres thick, and strong enough to support the weight of any person. I carried one piece of wood, and Zagero another, and in seconds we had a bridge over the crevasse, directly above Jackstraw and Helene. I tied a rope round myself and quickly lowered myself down from the bridge until I was standing on the snow bridge beside Jackstraw and Helene.

I called for another rope and tied this tightly around Helene's waist. The others above began to pull Helene up, and as I pushed her from below, I heard and felt the ice beginning to crack beneath my feet. I caught Jackstraw by the arm and we jumped over to the other side of the bridge. A second later the side where we had been standing fell down into the depths of the crevasse.

We squashed our bodies against the ice wall, scarcely daring to breathe. A sudden cry of pain from Helene, as she was pulled up over the edge of the crevasse, made me look up. It was then that I saw Corazzini. He was standing very close to the edge, and he had my gun in his hand.

I have never felt such bitterness and anger – and such fear. The one thing I had tried so hard to avoid – to have Jackstraw and myself both defenceless in front of the killers – had actually happened. Corazzini must have pushed Helene over the edge, knowing that one of us would not hesitate to go down after her to bring her to safety. I had helped his plans further by going down as well, the minute I realized that Jackstraw had broken his arm. Things could not have gone better for Corazzini.

Just as I was wondering how he was going to kill us, I saw the Reverend Smallwood moving towards him, his arms in the air, saying something that I couldn't hear. I saw Corazzini change his gun over to his left hand and hit Smallwood across the face. This was followed by the sound of a body falling on the ice.

Then Corazzini waved the others back with his gun and came towards the two pieces of wood bridging the crevasse. I immediately realized what he intended to do. Instead of wasting two bullets, he would simply kick the wood over the edge and leave us to fall to our death in the depths below.

I was trying to think of some last crazy way of jumping to safety when I felt a rope hit my shoulder. I looked up and saw Corazzini smiling down at me.

'Are you going to stay down there all day?' he said. 'Come on up.'

In the ninety seconds that it took for us to be lifted to safety I felt hope, amazement, relief, suspicion – all at the same time. I was shaking from head to toe but Corazzini pretended not to notice and stepped forward, putting the gun into my hand. 'You're a bit careless with your gun, Doc.'

'But . . . but why did you take it?' I asked, still confused and shaken.

'Because I've got a new job in Glasgow that I want to start,' he said sharply.

I knew what he meant. He was convinced, as I was, that someone had pushed Helene over deliberately. I could guess who that someone was.

My first thoughts were for Jackstraw. I took off his coat as carefully as I could and found, to my relief, that his arm wasn't actually broken – his elbow had just moved out of place. As I moved the bone back into place, his face showed no expression at all, but he broke into a smile when all was well again.

I walked over to Helene, who was still trembling from the shock. 'I don't know how to thank you both,' she said.

'Don't try,' I said. 'Who pushed you?'

She stared at me. 'What?'

'You heard me, Helene. Who did it?'

'Yes. I . . . I was pushed,' she admitted. 'But it was an accident. I know it was.'

'Who did it?' I continued.

Solly Levin spoke. 'It was me. It was an accident. I sort of tripped. Someone hit my foot and—'

'Who hit your foot?'

'For God's sake!' he cried out. 'Why would I want to do a thing like that?'

'I think you should tell me that,' I said, turning away. I walked back to the tractor and heard Corazzini say to Smallwood, 'I'm sorry I hit you, Reverend. I didn't really think you were one of the killers, but I couldn't take any risks.'

We continued our journey and crossed the rest of the Vindeby Nunataks without further trouble. We then stopped for a meal, but Margaret Ross, who was supposed to be preparing it, came up to me with a worried look in her eyes. 'The tins of meat, Dr Mason! I can't find them!'

'They must be there somewhere, Margaret,' I said. 'Come on, let's have a look.'

Without thinking, I had called her by her name, and a slight smile touched her lips. It was the first time I had ever seen her smile, and I felt my heart turn over. But this wasn't the right time to think of these things. We looked everywhere, but couldn't find the tins of meat. This was the opportunity I had been waiting for and I whispered in Jackstraw's ear.

Then I called the whole group together. 'Our last tins of meat have disappeared,' I announced. 'Somebody stole them. That person had better tell me, because I'm going to discover who it was anyway.'

There was silence. Then a sudden sharp sound made everyone turn, and behind them they saw Jackstraw, now aiming his rifle at Zagero's head. I brought out my gun and also pointed it at Zagero. 'Bring your bag here,' I said to him. 'Open it.'

'It's locked.'

'Unlock it.'

'I can't find the keys.'

I asked Corazzini to search Zagero because I wanted to keep both our guns pointed at him. Corazzini searched him but found nothing. I then asked Corazzini to search Solly Levin and, ten seconds later, he found a bunch of keys. Levin shouted out, 'He must have put them there. I never had those keys!'

'OK, Corazzini,' I said. 'Let's see what we can find.'

Corazzini opened Zagero's bag and under the first layer of clothes found three tins of meat.

'Tell me, Zagero,' I said coldly. 'Can you think of one good reason why I shouldn't kill you now?'

'You're making a really big mistake,' replied Zagero. 'Do you really think I'd have been such a fool as to put those tins there?'

My mind was made up. 'Tie up their feet,' I ordered. 'From now on Zagero and Levin will ride, with their feet tied, on the front of the tractor sledge – and with a gun on them all the time.'

Two hours later we stopped and set up the radio. For the first time I did not bother to move away from the tractor, so every word could be heard by the others. I tried to contact Uplavnik, but without success. I then contacted Hillcrest and told him that we had caught the two killers. My voice showed no excitement, not even relief. I think I was too exhausted, too depressed. I realized I had grown to like Zagero.

Hillcrest had no more information from Uplavnik about the passenger list or what the plane had been carrying. Various ships were making their way to Uplavnik and four planes were out looking for us.

As he spoke about their problems with the tractor and the petrol, I suddenly had an idea. 'Wait a minute,' I said. I went inside the cabin and over to Mahler's bed. 'Did you say you'd worked for an oil company?' I asked.

'Yes. Why?' His voice was weak and he breathed with difficulty.

I explained how Hillcrest had been trying to get the sugar out of the petrol. It didn't take Mahler long to think of a better way. 'If he's got a forty-litre container, tell him to pour out about eight litres of petrol and then pour in the same amount of water. Stir well. Wait for ten minutes and then pour off the top thirty-two litres, which will be almost pure petrol. Sugar doesn't dissolve in petrol, but it does in water. If you put in enough water, it will sink to the bottom, carrying the sugar with it.'

'As easy as that!' I said, amazed. 'Any more good ideas, Mr Mahler?'

'Yes. We're obviously carrying more fuel than we need. Why don't we leave some behind so that Captain Hillcrest can pick it up? In fact, why didn't you do that last night?'

I stared at him for a moment. 'I'll tell you why, Mr Mahler,' I said. 'It's because I'm the greatest fool the world has ever known.' And I returned to tell Hillcrest what a fool I was.

10

We drove without stopping through the whole of that evening and the following night. We dared not stop because the lives of Mahler and Marie LeGarde depended on our getting to the coast as soon as possible.

Mahler had lost consciousness just before nine o'clock and was now breathing with great difficulty. If we didn't get some insulin into him soon, he would be dead in two or three days. Marie LeGarde was also becoming dangerously weak.

While I was busy worrying about my patients, Jackstraw was worrying about the weather. It was now much warmer, the wind was growing stronger, and the skies were dark and heavy with fast-moving clouds of snow. All the conditions were right for one of Greenland's violent storms, when the winds could reach terrifying speeds.

We drove as fast as we could and were making very good progress, but by four in the morning, when we were about a hundred kilometres from Uplavnik and the coast, we came across a new difficulty – the *sastrugi*. These are waves in the frozen snow, caused by the winds. They go up and down like a stormy sea, forcing a tractor to move at a slow crawl. We carried on for four more hours and stopped at eight o'clock.

We had a small breakfast but by now I was so exhausted that it was hard for me to eat. I had had no sleep for almost three days, and I had to force myself to make radio contact with

Hillcrest, as we had agreed.

Everyone, except Mahler and Marie LeGarde, could hear my conversation with Hillcrest. They seemed to find comfort in hearing another human voice, although it was coming from such a distance.

'What news?' I asked eagerly.

'We're making excellent progress,' Hillcrest replied. 'The petrol idea worked wonderfully. We're approaching the Vindeby Nunataks and we'll be through them by this afternoon.' This was great news, but Hillcrest had more to tell us. 'We've finally got some official information about what you're carrying with you. It's valued at about a million pounds. That explains why the Government refused to say anything earlier on and why such a big search was started. The aircraft-carrier *Triton* is going to collect it personally.'

'For heaven's sake!' I shouted. 'What are you talking about? What was the plane carrying?'

'Sorry. It's a guided-missile mechanism, which is so advanced and so secret that only a few scientists in the whole of the United States know about it. It's the only one of its kind and was being sent to Britain so that it could be studied by scientists over there.'

He paused for a moment and then continued. 'I understand that both governments are prepared to do anything – anything at all – to recover this mechanism and prevent it from falling into the wrong hands. To help you recognize it, Dr Mason, I'm now going to describe it to you. It's disguised to look like a large portable metal radio with a leather strap handle. If you find that radio, Dr Mason, you'll—'

I never heard the end of that sentence. Zagero, at that exact moment, jumped up from his seat and, with his feet still tied, threw himself violently towards Corazzini, who was struggling to bring something out from under his coat. Corazzini moved quickly to one side, but Zagero's right arm shot out and hit Corazzini with such force that he fell to the ground like a matchstick. Never in my life had I seen such power. For a few seconds nobody spoke. Then I said in a whisper, 'So it was Corazzini, after all!'

'Of course it was Corazzini!' said Zagero. He put his hand under Corazzini's coat and, bringing out a gun, said, 'You'd better keep this, Doc. One day they'll probably find that this gun matches the marks on some very interesting bullets.'

He threw the gun over to me. I had never seen that type of gun before. I put it on the ground and pulled out my own gun, which I aimed at the unconscious Corazzini.

'But . . . but how did you know?' I said. 'How did you know it was him?'

'It had to be him. I knew it wasn't me. I knew it wasn't Solly. So it had to be Corazzini.'

'Yes. Of course. It had to be Corazzini.' It was hard for me to think clearly. My thoughts were in total confusion. Then an alarm bell began to ring in my mind. 'But there were two of them. Corazzini had someone helping him—'

I didn't get any further because a metal object suddenly hit my wrist with such force that it sent my gun flying. At the same time something small and hard dug violently into the back of my neck.

'Don't move, Dr Mason.' It was the Reverend Smallwood who spoke, but his voice was hard and controlled and no longer recognizable. 'Drop your gun, Jackstraw,' he ordered. 'If you make one move, I'll shoot Dr Mason.'

Corazzini was now on his feet again and was able to catch the gun Smallwood threw back to him. 'Get out, all of you!' Corazzini ordered. 'And hurry up!'

We carried Mahler and Marie LeGarde out of the tractor cabin and Smallwood waved us all into a straight line facing Corazzini and himself. Snow was beginning to fall quite heavily.

Then Smallwood called out to me. 'You haven't finished your radio call, Dr Mason. Finish it. Your friend Hillcrest will be wondering why there's been a delay. Be careful not to make him suspicious. Keep the call short.'

I kept it short. I made some excuse for the delay, and finished calmly, 'I'll call you again at noon, Captain Hillcrest. This is Mayday calling off. Mayday. Mayday.'

I switched off and had only moved one step away before Smallwood dug the gun into my stomach.

'Mayday? What's that?'

'It's the sign we use when we're ending a call,' I said.

'You're lying,' he said, looking at me with his cold, cruel eyes – the eyes of a killer.

'I'm not lying,' I said angrily.

'I'm going to kill you after I count five – one, two, three—'

'I'll tell you what it means!' The cry came from Margaret Ross. 'Mayday is the international air sign for calling for help in an emergency.' She broke down and cried. 'I had to tell him, Dr Mason. I had to. He was going to kill you.'

'Indeed I was,' Smallwood said icily. 'But I admire your courage, Dr Mason.'

'You'll never succeed, Smallwood,' I said. 'There are ships

and planes and thousands of men searching for you.'

'We'll see. Corazzini, get the box. Dr Mason, bring one of the maps from the driver's seat.'

When I brought the map, I found Corazzini sitting on the front of the tractor with Smallwood's case on his knees. He threw out the prayer books and the minister's clothes and then pulled out a metal box, which looked exactly like a tape-recorder. Except that it wasn't a tape-recorder. It was a much more complicated machine with a compass, and all sorts of switches and controls. Corazzini turned several switches, and soon a steady, high sound began to come from the machine.

He looked at Smallwood. 'We're receiving the signal perfectly. Direction 268,' he said.

Smallwood's face showed no emotion. These professionals had obviously planned every detail, with frightening efficiency. The metal box was clearly a radio direction-finder, and Corazzini had just picked up a pre-arranged radio signal from somewhere. Probably from a fishing-boat, or even a submarine, close to the shore, where their friends would be waiting for them.

Smallwood called out to me. 'Dr Mason, I want you to show me, on that map you've got there, our exact position.'

'You can go to hell,' I replied.

'Yes, I was expecting that. However, I'm not blind, and I've noticed that you've become rather fond of our stewardess, Miss Ross. If you don't do as you're told, I'll shoot her.'

I did not doubt him for a second. I told him our position, and Jackstraw, when asked, did so too. Our two answers, although given separately, were the same. Smallwood nodded to Corazzini. 'We're about a hundred kilometres from the foot of the Kangalak glacier—'

'Why the hell didn't you make the plane land there in the first place and save us all these problems?' I said.

Smallwood didn't give a direct answer. Instead he said, 'The captain deserved to die. I had ordered him to land on the coast near the Kangalak glacier where our . . . er, friends had discovered a place, five kilometres long and absolutely flat, which would have been an excellent place to land. It wasn't until I saw how high the plane was flying, just before the crash, that I realized that he had deceived me.' Then, looking at Corazzini, he said, 'Come on. We've got to start moving.'

'I suppose you're going to leave us here to starve and die of cold?' I said bitterly.

'I'm no longer interested in what happens to you,' he said. 'But we can't take the risk of you chasing after us. Corazzini, bring some rope from the sledge and tie their feet. Sit in the snow, all of you. OK, Corazzini. Tie up Dr Mason first.'

Corazzini gave his gun to Smallwood, came towards me and knelt down in the snow to start tying me up.

'No!' My voice was wild, desperate. 'Jackstraw, Zagero – all of you! Stand up if you want to live! Attack him if he starts shooting at one of us. He can't possibly kill us all, before we get him. We know too much about their plans. And if we let them tie us up, they can shoot us slowly, one by one – and there won't be a damn thing we can do to stop them!'

There was a moment's silence. Then Smallwood said, 'Dr Mason's right. He's not as stupid as I thought. We can't get rid of all of you at once. One of you, at least, will reach the cover of the snow and darkness. I think you'd better ride with us a little way.'

And this is what we did. For nine long hours of rising winds and heavy, driving snow. They were the longest fifty kilometres I've ever travelled. Corazzini drove all the time, while Smallwood sat in the back of the tractor cabin, his gun and a searchlight pointing at the rest of us, who were packed together on the tractor sledge, three metres away from him. Margaret and Helene had been taken into the tractor cabin, their hands tied together; they were being kept prisoners to ensure our good behaviour.

Soon after we had set off, Jackstraw put something in my hand and whispered, 'Corazzini's wallet. It fell from his pocket when Zagero knocked him down. He hasn't yet realized that he's lost it.'

In the torchlight I opened Corazzini's wallet and found inside the newspaper article that I had taken from the dead body of Colonel Harrison. I read it out aloud. Smallwood could not hear us over the roar of the wind and the tractor engine.

From my brief glance in the plane, I already knew it was about a disaster in New Jersey, where a passenger train had fallen over the edge of a bridge and plunged into the waters below, drowning a large number of passengers. The main facts in the article, however, were that the train had been carrying an army official, that he was one of the forty who had died, and that he had been carrying a 'super-secret guided-missile mechanism'.

There was a long silence which Jackstraw then broke by saying, 'So now we know why you were hit on the head.'

Zagero immediately interrupted. 'Hit on the head? What do you mean?'

I told him how I had found the newspaper article on Colonel Harrison's body and then how it had been taken from me.

We rode on the tractor sledge for nine long hours of rising winds and heavy, driving snow.

'But why were you hit on the head?' insisted Zagero. 'What difference would it have made if you had read the article?'

'Can't you see?' I said impatiently. 'The two disasters are so similar that I would have become suspicious. Then I heard from Hillcrest that something highly secret was being carried on the plane. And remember that I found the newspaper article on an army officer, who was almost certainly the person carrying the secret. If I'd known all this, I'd have examined everything in each person's luggage, including Corazzini's portable radio and that tape-recorder in Smallwood's case. God, how stupid I've been! How can you ever forgive me?'

'We've all been just as stupid,' Zagero was quick to add. 'It all seems so obvious now – why we crashed in the middle of nowhere, for instance. The captain must have known what was being carried on the plane and therefore decided to crash-land, risking our lives, in order to prevent Smallwood from reaching the coast.'

'Yes, and other things are obvious, too,' I said bitterly. 'How, and why, for instance, Corazzini pretended to throw a coin to choose who would sleep on the floor in the cabin. It was to give himself a chance to kill the radio operator in his sleep.'

'We all missed seeing things,' said Zagero. 'There was only one thing I actually knew and you didn't. Corazzini hit Smallwood by the crevasse in the pass in order to throw suspicion on me.'

There was a moment's silence as everyone put together the different pieces of information that we now knew. Then Solly Levin spoke. 'But how did the fire in the plane happen?'

'They knew that when Hillcrest found sugar in the petrol at our cabin, he would try to use the petrol in the plane,' I explained. 'So they started the fire to make sure that Hillcrest couldn't use the plane's petrol.'

After another silence Zagero spoke. 'I think I've got some explaining to do, too. It's about the behaviour of this chap next to me – Solly Levin.' Zagero put his hand on Levin's shoulder. 'He's my Dad, you see.'

'What? Your father?'

'That's right, Dr Mason,' Levin agreed. 'I use the name Levin instead of Zagero because boxers aren't allowed to have a close relation as their manager. It's not honest of me, I know, but it doesn't do any harm.'

'It did this time,' I said. 'If I'd known more about you both, I probably wouldn't have been suspicious about you. Then Corazzini and Smallwood would have been the only possible suspects left. However,' I went on bitterly, 'I expect I would have made some other stupid mistake.'

At five o'clock in the afternoon the tractor stopped, and Corazzini walked round to the cabin. He told Smallwood that the coast was now only fifty kilometres away. Smallwood looked at us. 'OK. This is where you get off. Out, all of you.'

We were so cold we could hardly move. 'Can't you at least leave us some food, a tent, and the dog sledge?' I said desperately. 'Mahler and Marie LeGarde can't walk at all.'

'You're wasting your time,' he said. 'Get out, all of you!'

Levin suddenly moaned in pain. 'I can't move. It's my legs! I think they're frozen.'

'Maybe a bullet in one of your legs will help,' Smallwood said coldly.

Immediately, Zagero moved towards Smallwood. 'Don't

touch him, Smallwood,' he warned. 'If you lay one finger on my old dad, I'll break your neck like a rotten carrot.' I believed him. So, I think, did Smallwood.

'Your Dad?' Smallwood said, thoughtfully. 'You mean this man's your father?'

Zagero nodded.

'Good. We'll exchange him for the German girl. No one cares about her.'

Levin was carried into the tractor cabin and Smallwood, turning to Helene, said, 'Get out!'

It was then that it happened. As Helene passed by Smallwood she tripped, and he put out an arm – either to help her or to push her away from him. She immediately kicked out wildly, knocking the gun out of his hand. Smallwood jumped after it like a cat, picked it up and aimed it straight at Helene, his eyes flashing with a mad anger. Mrs Dansby-Gregg screamed, 'Helene! Look out!' She rushed forward to push her maid to one side. Smallwood fired and the bullet caught Mrs Dansby-Gregg in the middle of her back. She fell face down in the frozen snow.

Smallwood nodded to Corazzini and got into the tractor, with his gun still aimed at us. Corazzini started the engine and moved off. We were left standing there, a lonely little group, with the dead woman at our feet, watching as the tractor, the tractor sledge, the dog sledge and the dogs disappeared into the darkness.

Only the German girl spoke. 'Helene!' she said in a strange voice. 'She called me Helene!' I looked at her, then stared unseeingly after the disappearing lights of the tractor.

11

The suffering that we experienced that night is a memory that will never die. How many hours did we walk, and struggle, after that tractor? Six hours, eight, ten? I shall never know. Time lost all meaning for us that night.

Anger and fear drove us onwards. The storm had grown worse, with a violent, screaming wind that carried with it a flying wall of snow and ice. It would have been impossible to walk into that wind, but it was blowing down the steep, narrow valley of the Kangalak glacier, so it beat on our bent and aching backs.

And ache our backs did. We had to carry the three who could no longer walk. The unconscious Mahler was carried, for hour after hour, by Zagero. I carried Marie LeGarde, who was now also unconscious, and Jackstraw carried Helene, who had fainted less than an hour after the tractor's disappearance. Brewster was weakening fast, but from time to time he bravely insisted on carrying one of the unconscious bodies for a short way, until he fell to his knees with exhaustion.

We would have died that night, just as Smallwood and Corazzini had intended, had it not been for Balto. The loyal Balto had not forgotten us. Soon after the tractor had left us, he came running out of the snow towards us and led us down the Kangalak glacier towards the coast.

Suddenly, sometime between midnight and three o'clock, he

86

stopped, gave a strange wolf-like call, listened for an answer and then changed direction. Three minutes later we came across the dog sledge. Smallwood had obviously found it too difficult to pull behind the tractor, and had therefore abandoned it.

With relief we put Mahler, Marie LeGarde and Helene onto the dog sledge, with Brewster sitting at the back, helping to support them. We moved off again into the darkness, with the three of us pulling the sledge over the smooth ice of the glacier. Our progress was no faster, however. The wind was now so strong and the snow so heavy that we soon had to stop, and wait until the blizzard had died down a little.

We dug into the snow to shelter from the wind and took the three unconscious people off the sledge. So great was my exhaustion that it was several seconds before I realized that Brewster was missing.

'Good God!' I shouted. 'The Senator! I'm going back to look for him.'

'No, you're not!' said Jackstraw. 'You'd never find your way back again.'

He sent Balto to look for the Senator and within two minutes Balto was back. We then followed Balto and found Brewster, lying face down in the snow, dead. The blizzard was already throwing a white blanket over him. Within an hour he would be buried deep beneath the snow. I didn't need to examine him. I knew that fifty years of over-eating and over-drinking would have made his heart dangerously weak. But this terrible journey had shown him to be a man of great determination and courage.

We lay, squashed together in our snow-hole, until the blizzard began to die down. At four in the morning I woke up and looked carefully at my companions one by one. Mahler, I was sure, was dying; he couldn't possibly live for more than twelve hours. Helene seemed to have lost all interest in living, but Marie LeGarde, at least, was conscious again. As for Zagero, his hands were now so badly damaged by frostbite that he would never fight as a boxer again.

We put the sick people on the sledge and set off again. By eight o'clock the storm was over, but our progress was still slow. The ice of the Kangalak glacier was now very rough and bumpy and full of cracks; we had to search for a safe route for the sledge between crevasses and great piles of ice-rocks. It was heart-breaking to think of Hillcrest, who must by now be very close to us. But without a radio there was no chance of us finding him, or him finding us.

At half-past eight in the morning we suddenly found the tractor sledge. It had obviously become too difficult for Smallwood and Corazzini to pull, and so they had left it there with all its contents – except, of course, for the radio. We wrapped Mahler and Marie LeGarde in the blankets that had been left on the sledge and started walking again. Then a thought suddenly hit me – a thought so amazing that I started laughing.

'My God! And I almost missed it!'

'Missed what, Doc?' said Zagero impatiently.

'Come back to the tractor sledge and see. Smallwood says he thinks of everything, but he's made his first really big mistake.'

We ran back to the sledge and there we saw, lying among our other scientific equipment, the two things that had caused my excitement and laughter. They were the magnesium flares, which we lit on expeditions to indicate our position on the ice-cap, and the radio-carrying balloons, which we filled with gas and sent up into the upper atmosphere to obtain special weather information.

'Just look at what we can do with these two things!' I shouted to Zagero. Jackstraw and I tied three magnesium flares to a balloon, filled the balloon with gas, lit the flares, and then sent the balloon into the dark sky. The flares burst into a brilliant ball of flame, more than a thousand metres above our heads.

'This,' breathed Zagero slowly, 'this is simply amazing.'

We sent up two more balloons with flares. No one could miss them. They would be seen by Hillcrest, by the ships off the coast, and by the searching planes. But then a horrible thought hit me. The flares would probably be seen by Corazzini and Smallwood as well. They would know that the hunt was closing in on them. They were killers, and now they would become frightened, desperate killers. And they had Zagero's father and Margaret with them.

But we had no choice. Mahler and Marie LeGarde were also close to death. The third flare burst into flame and I closed my eyes against its brightness for a second.

Then I felt Jackstraw's hand on my arm. Looking at his face, I saw the biggest smile I had seen for weeks. I followed the direction of his pointing arm and there, shining in the sky, was the red and white flare of a rocket. Our call for help had been answered!

No sight had ever seemed as wonderful as that single rocket in the sky – not even the sight, twenty minutes later, of Hillcrest's large and modern snow-tractor as it appeared over the top of a small hill. We waved like madmen as soon as we saw it, and although we only had to wait ten minutes until it arrived, those few minutes seemed endless.

Soon, we were all inside the warmth and comfort of Hillcrest's wonderfully equipped tractor. Within minutes, Mahler, Marie LeGarde and Helene were in warm, comfortable beds. There were hot drinks, plates of hot food – and a most welcome glass of whisky. There was no time to relax, however.

'A plane will be flying over us soon,' Hillcrest explained rapidly. 'It'll be carrying insulin for Mahler. We're going to fire three rockets and then light a magnesium flare in the place where we want the insulin to be dropped. Mahler will have his first injection in less than half an hour.'

This was wonderful news, but now my other worries returned in force. I told Hillcrest our story, as briefly as possible. When I finished, he had already made up his mind. 'Well, if Smallwood and Corazzini are not far ahead of us, we'll drive like crazy down the glacier and catch them – and the secret mechanism.'

'No, we won't,' I said urgently. 'If they see us chasing them, Margaret and Levin will probably get a bullet through their heads. And by the way, Levin is Zagero's father. Look, what we must do is stay out of sight and move along, parallel with the glacier, but one or two kilometres away from their tractor. We'll get in front of them, and then, where the sides of the glacier valley become flatter and the ice becomes smoother, we'll hide and ambush them.'

'But we'll still have to fight them. They can still hold a gun against the heads of Levin and the stewardess,' Hillcrest said, frowning.

'There'll be no fight,' I said quietly. 'They'll almost certainly stay on the left-hand side of the glacier – it's easier driving there

– and they'll come into sight about fifty metres away from where we'll be hiding. Jackstraw will shoot Corazzini first – he'll probably be driving – then Smallwood. With Jackstraw's long-distance rifle and his skill at shooting, he can't possibly miss them.'

'But you can't do that,' said Hillcrest in horror. 'That's murder!' Turning to Jackstraw, he said, 'Are you really prepared to do that?'

'It will be a pleasure,' Jackstraw said very softly.

Hillcrest stared at us, but then Joss interrupted, saying that it was time to receive Mahler's insulin. Only seconds after we had sent up the flare, two parcels were dropped from a plane. I ran out and picked them up. Mahler's life had now been saved.

For two hours we drove over the difficult and dangerous ground on the slopes above the glacier valley, turning often to avoid the deep crevasses. At noon, the driver stopped. We had come round a cliff in the ice and could now see the smooth ice-cap stretching down to the coast. Nearby, the Kangalak glacier, here three hundred metres wide, curved away to the sea – the ice-filled waters of Baffin Bay. In the distance I could see two ships close to the shore. One was obviously the British aircraft-carrier, but it was the other ship which caught my attention. It was a fishing-boat and had no flag. I looked at it again, through the binoculars . . . and shouted to Joss.

'Are you still in radio contact with the aircraft-carrier?'

Joss nodded.

'Tell them there's a group of ten or twelve men coming onto the shore from a fishing-boat. They're probably carrying guns. I'm quite sure that they're going to move up the glacier. Ask for a group of our men to be sent on shore after them – fast!'

91

Just then came Hillcrest's excited shout from outside. 'We can hear their tractor coming!'

Jackstraw, Hillcrest and I hid behind some ice-rocks and, with our rifles ready, waited. The tractor was still a long way off. The success of our plan depended on their tractor coming down the same side of the glacier that we were on. I looked across at Jackstraw. His face, as cold as the glacier itself, showed no emotion. Hillcrest, on the other hand, was looking worried and unhappy. He didn't like murder. Neither did I. But then this wasn't murder. It was life-saving. Saving the lives of Margaret and Solly Levin.

Jackstraw lay in the snow and aimed his rifle, ready to shoot. And then, suddenly, the tractor had come into sight and Jackstraw was gently lowering his rifle. I had taken a gamble and I had lost it. The tractor was on the far side of the glacier. Smallwood and Corazzini were more than three hundred metres away. It was impossible to shoot them.

12

Desperately, I tried to think of a new plan. The killers would keep Margaret and Levin alive until the last moment, in order to prevent an attack. But once they were on their fishing-boat, what chance for Margaret and Levin then? Why bother to keep them alive?

My thoughts were interrupted by Hillcrest saying, 'I think those two killers are going to beat us after all.'

'Well, that's what you wanted, wasn't it?' I said bitterly.

'What I wanted! Good God, that missile mechanism—'

'Damn the missile mechanism!' I exploded. 'Let them keep it! In six months' time scientists will have invented something twice as good and much more secret.'

Hillcrest looked at me, shocked. Zagero, who had just joined us, said fiercely, 'I couldn't agree with you more, Doc. Who cares about their damned war-toys? My old man's out there on that tractor. And your girl.'

'His girl?' Hillcrest turned, looked at me for a long moment and then murmured, 'Sorry, Peter. I hadn't understood.'

Joss came running up at that moment. He was so excited that he had forgotten to put on his gloves and hat. 'The aircraft-carrier has sent some men ashore. Their boat's landing now. And in a few minutes' time four or five planes will be taking off. They're going to bomb the fishing-boat if Smallwood gets away with that missile mechanism.'

Five seconds later we heard a loud noise. It was coming from the engine of the tractor across the glacier. Corazzini, who was driving, must have seen or heard something that alarmed him. He was now going at top speed – the speed of a madman. No normal driver would have driven so fast over that steeply sloping crevasse ice.

I decided on a last, desperate gamble. If they continued driving the tractor at that speed, they would either kill themselves on the glacier or, if they got to the bottom safely and reached Baffin Bay, they would then kill Margaret and Levin.

'Can you stop the tractor?' I asked Jackstraw.

He nodded, his eyes on me. I nodded back.

But Zagero protested, 'You can't do that! They'll kill them! They'll kill them! My God, Mason, if you're really fond of that girl, you'd never—'

'Shut up!' I said fiercely, hurriedly picking up my rifle and some rope. 'If you think they'd ever let your father come out of this alive, you must be crazy.'

A second later I was running out onto the ice, bending low as Jackstraw's bullets screamed past me. The first one smashed straight into the engine, but still the tractor went on.

Hillcrest, Joss, Zagero and two of Hillcrest's men were now following me. I rushed on, leaping over the cracks in the ice. Jackstraw's bullets continued to hammer into the tractor, but that engine was tough.

Suddenly, when we were less than a hundred metres away, the tractor stopped, as Corazzini pushed down hard on the brakes. Something violent was obviously going on in the tractor, and as we got nearer, we could see what it was. Corazzini and Solly Levin were fighting fiercely. Levin had thrown himself on top of Corazzini and was hitting him in the face with the top of his bald head. Then the door on the driver's side burst open and the two men fell out, still fighting violently. I could see that Levin's hands were tied behind his back. The brave old man had been attacking Corazzini with his head alone. It was an act of desperate courage.

As we approached, Corazzini brought out his gun and aimed directly at Levin. Even as I threw myself at Corazzini and sent him flying, I knew that I was too late. Solly Levin was lying on the ice, a little blood-stained figure. There was no sign of movement from him.

I felt myself being pushed to one side as Johnny Zagero stared down at the man lying at his feet. For three long, terrible seconds Zagero stood there without moving. When he turned to Corazzini, his face was empty of all expression.

Corazzini started to run, but Zagero was faster and threw himself onto Corazzini like a tiger. The two men crashed to the ground together, kicking and clawing and hitting each other like madmen.

'Drop that gun!' It was Smallwood's iron voice. I turned quickly to see the pale, frightened face of Margaret Ross, and Smallwood's face, hardly visible, looking out from behind her shoulder.

'Drop your guns! Both of you! Drop them now!'

I hesitated, glancing at Hillcrest. Then there was the sound of a shot and a cry of pain from Margaret. He had shot her in her left arm, just below the elbow.

'Quick!' insisted Smallwood. 'The next bullet'll go through her shoulder.'

We dropped our rifles and, obeying his orders again, kicked

them over the edge of the nearest crevasse. We stood and watched as Corazzini and Zagero rolled over and over on the ice, first one on top, then the other. Smallwood had his gun pointed at them waiting for the second when the two men would move far enough apart for him to shoot Zagero.

Zagero was at a disadvantage. He was exhausted by the terrible night's walk and his frostbitten hands were covered in thick bandages. But those damaged hands were steadily hammering the life out of Corazzini with a power that was frightening.

As we stood watching the bitter fight, Hillcrest suddenly caught my arm. 'He's moving, Mason! He's alive!' He was pointing down at Solly Levin. Kneeling down to examine Levin, I found that he was, indeed, still breathing. By some amazing piece of luck he had escaped death, and was only suffering from a head injury.

The two men were still fighting. Suddenly Corazzini tore himself free and ran in the direction of some rocks. Zagero, cat-like, ran after him, moving so fast that Smallwood's bullet missed him. A gasp of pain came from Corazzini as once more Zagero knocked him down. The unseen battle continued behind the rocks, and we could hear the sound of bodies crashing and slipping on the ice. Seconds later, there came a sudden, desperate scream, followed by a long moan of pain. Then silence.

Zagero came out from behind the rocks, his face cut and bruised, his bandaged hands covered with blood.

'Finished?' I asked.

'Finished.'

'Good. Your father's still alive, Johnny. He's got a head

injury, that's all.'

With a look of joy spreading over his face, Zagero dropped down on his knees beside Solly Levin. I saw Smallwood aim his gun at Zagero's back.

'Don't do it, Smallwood!' I shouted. 'You'll have only three bullets left.'

Smallwood turned and stared at me with the cold, flat eyes of a killer. Then he understood, and nodded. He might need those bullets later. He turned to Jackstraw, the nearest to him. 'Bring out my radio from the tractor cabin,' he ordered. 'Leave it here and join your friends – while I join mine.' He nodded down the glacier. 'Or hadn't you noticed?'

We hadn't. But we noticed them now. The first man from the fishing-boat had reached the foot of the glacier. A few seconds later six or seven of them were climbing up the slippery ice. Smallwood smiled. 'There's my welcoming party. You'll all remain here while Miss Ross and I go down to meet them. Don't move.'

He had won. Within seconds he would be safe. He bent down to pick up his radio, then turned to stare up at the sky.

I had heard the noise too, and I knew what it was before Smallwood did. It was coming from four planes that were flying low, forming a circle above us.

'They're our planes, Smallwood,' I said fiercely. 'We called for them by radio. They've got orders to shoot and destroy any person going down the glacier – any person, especially, with a case or radio in his hand.' It was a lie, but Smallwood didn't know that.

'The planes can stay there for as long as they like,' he said calmly. 'They won't touch me as long as I stay close to you. And in an hour it will be dark, after which I can leave safely.'

'Why don't you give in, Smallwood?' I said. I had no hope of persuading this madman, but I kept on talking. I had to keep on talking because I had just seen something, and it was essential that he didn't turn and see it too. 'Listen, Smallwood. Those planes are also carrying bombs. And do you know why, Smallwood?'

Twelve men were moving quietly across the ice towards us, from the other side of the glacier. Our men, from the aircraft-carrier. They were probably Marines, and they were carrying powerful guns.

'Because they're going to make sure you never leave this glacier alive, Smallwood.'

Why were they moving so slowly? I needed to hold his attention for another thirty seconds.

'They're going to destroy that fishing-boat, Smallwood.'

Smallwood's welcoming party, who were still some distance away down the glacier, had seen the approaching Marines and were now shouting and waving their arms. I tried to speak more loudly, hoping that Smallwood wouldn't hear them. But it was too late. Smallwood heard their shouts, turned round, and saw the Marines. His face and voice changed. He was now more like a wild animal than a man.

'Who are they?' he demanded. 'What are they doing?'

'They've been ordered to get that missile mechanism from you,' I replied. 'They'll kill you if necessary. This is the end, Smallwood. Give up your gun.'

Smallwood swore violently and, pushing Margaret in front of him, jumped into the driving cabin of the tractor. I threw myself at the tractor door, shouting, 'You madman! You'll kill yourself, you'll kill the girl—'

His gun coughed softly. I felt a burning pain in my arm and I crashed backwards onto the ice as Smallwood released the brakes. At once the tractor began to move and Jackstraw leapt forward just in time to pull me away from those huge wheels.

The next moment I was running again, with Jackstraw behind me. The glacier was so steep and slippery here that the tractor was completely out of control. It slid violently, first to one side and then another. Soon it spun round in a complete half–circle and started sliding backwards down the glacier, approaching some big rocks further down with frightening speed.

Jackstraw and I were a hundred metres behind the tractor when it hit an ice-hill, spun round several times and then went straight into one of the biggest rocks. We saw Smallwood and Margaret fall out of the driving cabin – Smallwood still holding the radio. Then they slipped and fell, and disappeared down a crevasse. Almost immediately afterwards Jackstraw and I threw ourselves down onto the ice as we heard the loud roar of gunfire. Two planes were flying low across the glacier, with red fire shooting from their guns. Further down we saw the men from the fishing-boat turn and run for shelter.

I was now ten metres ahead of Jackstraw and soon, mad with fear, I reached the crevasse where Smallwood and Margaret had disappeared. It was less than a metre wide, and as I looked over the side I saw, with enormous relief, that it was only five metres deep. At the bottom was a solid shelf of rock on which Smallwood and Margaret were standing.

Smallwood looked up at me, pressed his gun fiercely against Margaret's forehead, and said softly, 'A rope, Mason. Get me a rope. This crevasse is closing. The ice is moving.'

He wasn't lying this time. All glaciers moved, and I knew that some of the ones on the coast of West Greenland moved with amazing speed. And at that moment I felt the ice move slightly under my feet.

'Hurry up!' His voice was urgent, but controlled. 'Hurry up or I'll kill her!'

I knew that he meant it.

'OK,' I said calmly. I took the rope off my shoulder and held it up. 'Here it comes.'

He held out both hands to catch the falling rope. I stepped forward, jumped and fell on top of him with all my weight. There was nothing that he could do. The crevasse was so narrow that he couldn't move aside to avoid me.

We crashed together onto the shelf of rock and I locked my hands around his throat, knocking his head against the side of the crevasse. He kicked and struggled violently, but I held on until he was too weak to fight back.

The ice was moving fast. The two walls of the crevasse were now only forty-five centimentres apart. Margaret was already safe. Jackstraw had been lowered down into the crevasse by Hillcrest and his men. He had fastened a rope around her, and the two of them had been pulled to safety.

I was weak and dazed, but I heard Jackstraw shouting, as he threw down a rope, 'Quickly, Dr Mason! It'll close any second now!'

'I'm coming,' I answered. 'But throw down another rope for the missile mechanism. We can't leave it now – not after all we've suffered.'

Twenty seconds later, as I climbed over the edge of the

'A rope, Mason. Get me a rope. This crevasse is closing,' said Smallwood.

crevasse, the ice moved another five centimetres and we heard Smallwood's voice. 'Throw me a rope. For God's sake, throw me a rope.'

I thought of the number of people who had died because of Smallwood – the plane's captain, the other three officers, Colonel Harrison, Senator Brewster and Mrs Dansby-Gregg. I thought, too, of the people who had almost died because of him – Mahler and Marie LeGarde. I thought also of how often he had threatened death to the girl now trembling in my arms. Then I looked at Jackstraw, who held a rope in his hands, and I saw in his face the same cold, unforgiving anger that was in my own mind. And then Jackstraw moved towards the edge of the crevasse, lifted the whole coil of rope high above his head, threw it down onto the man below, and stepped back without a word.

We turned, Jackstraw and I, and walked slowly up the glacier to meet the Marines, supporting Margaret Ross between us. As we walked, we felt the glacier shiver and the ice moved once again under our feet.

GLOSSARY

aircraft-carrier a large warship which carries planes and is used for landing and taking off

ambush *(v)* to make a surprise attack from a hidden position

antenna a wire or pole for sending and receiving radio messages

arctic referring to the very cold regions around the North Pole

balloon a large light bag filled with gas to make it rise in the air

binoculars an instrument with special glass for each eye, which makes distant objects seem nearer

blizzard a very bad snowstorm

boxer someone who boxes as a sport (fighting with hands in gloves)

cabin a small building or shelter; or a small room on a plane or other vehicle

cabinet a case or container for a radio, television, etc.

coil a long piece of rope, wound up into a number of circles

collar-bone a bone joining the breastbone and the shoulder-blade

compartment one of the rooms into which a plane or train is divided

compass an instrument for finding direction, with a needle that points to magnetic north

crevasse a deep, open crack in the ice of a glacier

crushed pressed or squashed so hard that there is damage or injury

damn/damned *(informal)* words used to express annoyance, anger, etc.

dazed confused and unable to think clearly

diabetic a person suffering from diabetes, a disease in which there is too much sugar in the blood

explosive *(n)* a substance that is likely or able to explode

frostbite injury to the body, especially fingers and toes, caused by extreme cold

fuse a long piece of easily burnt material that can carry fire to a bomb or explosive, so that it explodes

glacier a river of ice that moves slowly down a valley

guided-missile mechanism an electronic instrument which can guide a war rocket to its destination while in flight

hissing a sound like a long 's'

homing spool a length of rope or wire, wound round a circular object, which is used to find the way back to 'home' or a starting point

ice-cap a permanent covering of ice, especially in regions around the North and South Poles

injection putting a liquid into the body using a needle

insulin a substance produced in the body, which controls how the body uses sugar (diabetics have to have insulin injections)

leap *(v)* to jump or move very quickly

magnesium flare a very bright light made by burning magnesium, a silver-white metal

maid a female servant

Marines a group of soldiers trained to fight on land or sea

moan *(v)* to make a long, low sound of pain or suffering

pass *(n)* a route through a gap or low point in mountains

portable can be easily carried

radiator a metal case containing water, used for cooling the engine of a vehicle

Reverend a title used for a Church of England priest

ridiculous very silly; deserving to be laughed at

rifle a type of gun with a long barrel, which is usually fired from the shoulder

Senator a member of the American Senate, one of the two law-making parts of the government

shiver *(v)* to tremble from cold

signal *(n)* a sound or action which gives a message, command, etc.

sledge a vehicle with pieces of wood, metal, etc. instead of wheels, for travelling over ice and snow

sleeping-bag a large thick bag of warm material to sleep in when camping

stewardess a woman who serves passengers on a plane

stove a piece of equipment for cooking or heating rooms

stretcher a simple bed of poles and a piece of material, for carrying a sick or injured person in a lying position

tank a large container for petrol, oil, etc.

tape-recorder an instrument which can record and play back sound

transmitter an instrument for sending radio signals

trap-door a door in a floor, ceiling or roof

windscreen a glass window in the front of a vehicle or plane

Before Reading

1 Read the story introduction on the first page of the book, and the back cover. How much do you know now about the story? For each sentence, circle Y (Yes) or N (No).

  1 This story happens near the South Pole. Y/N

  2 The men at the weather station are used to working in very cold conditions. Y/N

  3 An airliner has crashed near the weather station. Y/N

  4 Peter Mason was a passenger on the plane. Y/N

  5 There were fifteen people on the plane. Y/N

  6 Four people on the plane were shot. Y/N

  7 The radio is broken. Y/N

2 What do you think will happen in the story? For each sentence, circle Y (Yes) or N (No).

  1 Someone will be lost in a terrible snowstorm. Y/N

  2 There will not be enough food for everyone. Y/N

  3 One of the passengers will have a serious illness. Y/N

  4 Peter Mason will fall in love with someone. Y/N

  5 Soldiers will come and rescue the passengers. Y/N

  6 One of the scientists will be shot. Y/N

  7 Two more of the plane passengers will die. Y/N

  8 There will be more than one killer. Y/N

  9 The killer(s) will be shot. Y/N

  10 The killer(s) will escape. Y/N

While Reading

Read Chapters 1 and 2, and then answer these questions.

1 How long had Dr Mason been working in Greenland?
2 Why did Jackstraw think it was a big plane that he heard?
3 How did Dr Mason know that the plane was going to land?
4 How did the scientists carry the things needed for the rescue?
5 What did the scientists use to guide them over the snow?
6 Why was Dr Mason surprised to see the words 'British Airways' on the plane?
7 How many dead bodies did Dr Mason find before he went into the passenger compartment?
8 How many dead bodies did he find in the passenger compartment?
9 Why was it odd that the passengers weren't wearing seatbelts?
10 Who did they take back to the cabin first?
11 Who stayed behind to help Dr Mason when the other passengers went back to the cabin?
12 Why were the scientists angry that the radio was broken?

Read Chapter 3. Match the names of the passengers with the words and phrases, and then write a sentence about each one.

Example: The elderly woman, Marie LeGarde, was a famous actress.

Senator Brewster / Nick Corazzini / Mrs Dansby-Gregg / Helene Fleming / Marie LeGarde / Solly Levin / Theodore Mahler / Joseph Smallwood / Johnny Zagero

actress	minister	American politician
society woman	elderly woman	expensively dressed
boxer	little man	dark-haired young man
maid	famous	broken collar-bone
Jewish	boxer's manager	thin and elderly
businessman	priest's collar	white hair and moustache
cut forehead	German	

Before you read Chapter 4, can you guess what will happen? For each sentence, circle Y (Yes) or N (No).

1 The radio operator will die. Y/N
2 The passengers will wait in the cabin to be rescued. Y/N
3 Joss will find another radio that they can use. Y/N
4 They will leave the cabin and travel towards the coast. Y/N
5 They will discover that one of the dead men had a gun. Y/N
6 Dr Mason will think that Margaret Ross is a killer. Y/N

Read Chapters 4 to 6. Who said this, and to whom? What were they talking about?

1 'Won't they worry if they don't hear from you?'
2 'And why didn't you show it to me yesterday?'
3 'Somebody, out there, has just tried to murder me.'
4 'I don't suppose you know anything about this, by any chance?'
5 'Now, do you trust me?'
6 'Do you think we'll ever get there?'
7 'We know you're serious.'
8 'What on earth's happening out there?'
9 '. . . the fire in the plane explains one thing, at least.'
10 'I found a last handful of it lying on the floor of the tunnel.'

Read Chapters 7 and 8. Are these sentences true (T) or false (F)? Rewrite the false ones with the correct information.

1 Mahler stole all the sugar.
2 The sugar would save Mahler's life.
3 Dr Mason thought that Zagero was one of the killers.
4 The criminals started a fire in the toilet of the plane so that they could drug the passengers' coffee.
5 No one was standing near Margaret Ross when the radio fell and broke.
6 Everyone slept when they stopped the tractor.
7 Captain Hillcrest returned to the cabin to pick up more petrol.
8 Dr Mason told the other passengers that Hillcrest was only 130 kilometres behind them.
9 Someone took the gun from Dr Mason's pocket when he was hit on the head.
10 Hillcrest had travelled 32 kilometres since noon.

Before you read Chapters 9 and 10, can you guess what happens?

1 Someone falls into a crevasse. Is it . . .
   a) Helene?
   b) Corazzini?
   c) Levin?
2 Someone has something hidden in their bag. Is it . . .
   a) a gun?
   b) food?
   c) insulin?
3 The important thing being carried on the plane was . . .
   a) a piece of secret military equipment.
   b) a new sort of medicine.
   c) secret government papers.

4 The captain crashed the plane near the weather station . . .
  a) because he was lost.
  b) because the killers shot him.
  c) to stop the criminals from meeting their friends.
5 Someone else is going to be killed. Is it . . .
  a) Helene?
  b) Mrs Dansby-Gregg?
  c) Margaret Ross?
6 Decide which of these people are definitely not the two criminals, and which might be.
  a) Senator Brewster   e) Solly Levin
  b) Nick Corazzini   f) Theodore Mahler
  c) Mrs Dansby-Gregg   g) Reverend Smallwood
  d) Helene Fleming   h) Johnny Zagero

Read Chapters 11 and 12. Choose the best question-word for these questions and then answer them.

How / What / Which / Who / Why

1 . . . three people could no longer walk?
2 . . . did Balto find between midnight and three o'clock?
3 . . . died and fell off the sledge?
4 . . . did they find in the morning?
5 . . . two things on the sledge made Dr Mason happy?
6 . . . was going to shoot Corazzini and Smallwood?
7 . . . was it impossible to shoot them?
8 . . . did Levin attack Corazzini?
9 . . . killed Corazzini?
10 . . . didn't Smallwood shoot Zagero?
11 . . . did Smallwood try to escape in the tractor?
12 . . . did Dr Mason stop Smallwood shooting Margaret?

After Reading

1 **What did the killers do, and why? Fill in their names and make as many sentences as you can from the table.**

They	shot tried to shoot stole destroyed	the chief pilot Mrs Dansby-Gregg Colonel Harrison Solly Levin the fuse wire Helene the sugar Margaret Ross the radio	because . . . to . . .

2 **Put these sentences into the right order. Then put them together to make a paragraph. Use linking words (*and, but, so, when,* etc.) and pronouns (*he, she, it, who,* etc.) instead of names where possible.**

1 Mason thought that Corazzini was going to kill them.
2 Corazzini smiled and threw down a rope.
3 Mason lowered himself into the crevasse to help them.
4 Helene landed on a snow and ice bridge six metres down.
5 Mason and Jackstraw jumped to the other side of the bridge.
6 Mason heard the ice beginning to crack.
7 Helene slipped and fell into a crevasse.
8 Mason looked up.
9 Jackstraw jumped down after her.
10 Helene was then pulled to safety.
11 Mason tied a rope round Helene.

12 One side of the snow bridge collapsed.

13 Jackstraw hurt his arm as he fell.

14 Mason saw Corazzini with a gun in his hand.

Now write a paragraph about what happened when Smallwood and Margaret fell into the crevasse.

3 **Complete the conversation that Captain Hillcrest had with Joss. Use as many words as you like.**

Joss: Hillcrest, what on earth are you doing back here?

Hillcrest: We heard from Uplavnik _____.

Joss: Well, I can't tell you how glad I am to see you!

Hillcrest: It's good to see you too. But where _____.

Joss: They're _____.

Hillcrest: Why do I have to go after them? I _____.

Joss: You don't have to search for the plane.

Hillcrest: Why not? What do you mean?

Joss: It's _____.

Hillcrest: My God! What _____?

Joss: Most of them were OK. But _____.

Hillcrest: Dead? Oh no! But why didn't you radio for help?

Joss: _____.

Hillcrest: Are you sure? Let me have a look at it.

Joss: Look. It's smashed. There's something very strange going on. Mason and I believe _____.

Hillcrest: Murderers? That's crazy! Why do you think that?

Joss: _____.

Hillcrest: So Mason and Jackstraw are out there with a couple of killers? Why didn't they just wait here for help?

Joss: _____.

Hillcrest: Well, we'd better go after them right now. . .

4 Complete this paragraph about how Mrs Dansby-Gregg changed towards Helene. Use one word in each gap.

Helene worked for Mrs Dansby-Gregg as her _____. At first, Mrs Dansby-Gregg called her _____, not Helene. She didn't seem to realize that Helene's _____ was broken in the crash, and when she found out, she wasn't very _____. The next morning, she told her maid to get her a cup of _____, although Helene was _____. But later in the story, her feelings changed and she showed great _____ for Helene. She called her by her _____ name and when _____ tried to shoot her, she _____ her life.

Now write a similar paragraph about how Dr Mason changed towards Margaret Ross.

5 What might have happened if...? Complete these sentences in your own words.

1 If the pilot had landed near the Kangalak glacier, _____.
2 If they had had more food, _____.
3 If they had all stayed in the cabin, _____.
4 If Mason hadn't found one of the antenna poles when he was lost in the snow, _____.
5 If Corazzini and Smallwood hadn't set fire to the plane, _____.
6 If Corazzini and Smallwood hadn't put sugar in the petrol, _____.
7 If Mason had read the newspaper article earlier, _____.
8 If Mahler hadn't worked for an oil company, _____.
9 If Mason had known that Levin was Zagero's father, _____.

6 **Do you agree (A) or disagree (D) with these statements? Explain why.**

  1 Leaving Smallwood in the crevasse was revenge, not justice, and so was a criminal act.
  2 Shooting Corazzini and Smallwood on the tractor, even to save Solly Levin and Margaret Ross, would have been murder, as Hillcrest said.
  3 Solly Levin and Johnny Zagero should have revealed the fact that they were father and son.
  4 Mahler should not have stolen the sugar.
  5 Mrs Dansby-Gregg should have helped to bandage Helene's shoulder.

7 **Which of the people in this story did you most admire, and why? Who did you think was bravest? Write a few sentences about two or three of the characters.**

8 **Imagine that your plane has crash-landed in the Arctic. Which of these things would you need, and why? Choose the five most important ones. Would you add anything else to the list?**

balloons	gun	stretcher
bandages	insulin	snow sticks
compass	magnesium flare	sugar
dogs	petrol	tape recorder
food	radio	tent
explosive	rope	torch
fuse wire	sledge	tractor
guided-missile mechanism	sleeping-bag	warm clothes
homing spool	stove	

ABOUT THE AUTHOR

Alistair MacLean was born in Glasgow, Scotland, in 1922. He was the son of a church minister and was brought up in the Scottish Highlands. In 1941, during the Second World War, he left school and joined the Royal Navy. After the war he obtained a degree in English literature at Glasgow University and then became a schoolteacher, but in 1954 he won a short story competition run by the *Glasgow Herald* newspaper, and was invited by a publisher to write a novel.

His first novel, *HMS Ulysses* (1955), soon became a bestseller. It was based on his wartime experiences at sea and tells the terrifying story of a warship and the brave men who fought and died in the icy waters of the Atlantic Ocean. After the success of his next war story, *The Guns of Navarone* (1957), he gave up teaching and became a full-time writer.

MacLean preferred to call his books 'adventure stories' rather than novels, and they are certainly full of excitement. Brave men fight their enemies, in conditions of great physical difficulty, all over the world: from the cold Atlantic of his first novel to the heat of the South Seas in *South by Java Head* (1958); from the icy polar regions in *Night Without End* (1959) and *Ice Station Zebra* (1963) to the warmth of Florida in *Fear is the Key* (1961). In all, he wrote over twenty such stories, most of which sold over a million copies. Many of them, such as *Where Eagles Dare* (1967), were made into successful films.

Alistair MacLean also wrote spy stories, and biographies of T. E. Lawrence and Captain Cook. He was awarded a D. Litt. by Glasgow University in 1983, and died in 1987.

ABOUT BOOKWORMS

OXFORD BOOKWORMS LIBRARY
Classics • True Stories • Fantasy & Horror • Human Interest
Crime & Mystery • Thriller & Adventure

The OXFORD BOOKWORMS LIBRARY offers a wide range of original and adapted stories, both classic and modern, which take learners from elementary to advanced level through six carefully graded language stages:

Stage 1 (400 headwords)	**Stage 4** (1400 headwords)
Stage 2 (700 headwords)	**Stage 5** (1800 headwords)
Stage 3 (1000 headwords)	**Stage 6** (2500 headwords)

More than fifty titles are also available on cassette, and there are many titles at Stages 1 to 4 which are specially recommended for younger learners. In addition to the introductions and activities in each Bookworm, resource material includes photocopiable test worksheets and Teacher's Handbooks, which contain advice on running a class library and using cassettes, and the answers for the activities in the books.

Several other series are linked to the OXFORD BOOKWORMS LIBRARY. They range from highly illustrated readers for young learners, to playscripts, non-fiction readers, and unsimplified texts for advanced learners.

Oxford Bookworms Starters	*Oxford Bookworms Factfiles*
Oxford Bookworms Playscripts	*Oxford Bookworms Collection*

Details of these series and a full list of all titles in the OXFORD BOOKWORMS LIBRARY can be found in the *Oxford English* catalogues. A selection of titles from the OXFORD BOOKWORMS LIBRARY can be found on the next pages.

The Enemy

DESMOND BAGLEY

Retold by Ralph Mowat

On a beautiful summer evening in the quiet town of Marlow, a young woman is walking home from church. She passes a man who is looking at the engine of his car. He turns round, smiles at her . . . and throws acid into her face.

Then her father, the scientist George Ashton, disappears. And her sister, Penny, discovers that her husband-to-be, Malcolm, is a government agent. Why has Ashton disappeared, and why is Malcolm told to hunt for him? Who *is* George Ashton, anyway?

And who is the enemy?

Deadheads

REGINALD HILL

Retold by Rosalie Kerr

An English rose garden on a summer's day. A small boy watches with interest as his great-aunt cuts the deadheads off the rosebushes with a sharp knife. What could be more peaceful, more harmless?

Young Patrick grows up to be a calm, pleasant man, with a good job, a wife and two children, and the best rose garden for miles around. When somebody tells the police that Patrick Aldermann is killing people, Chief Superintendent Dalziel thinks it's probably all nonsense. But Inspector Pascoe is not sure . . .

American Crime Stories

RETOLD BY JOHN ESCOTT

'Curtis Colt didn't kill that liquor store woman, and that's a fact. It's not right that he should have to ride the lightning – that's what prisoners call dying in the electric chair. Curtis doesn't belong in it, and I can prove it.' But can Curtis's girlfriend prove it? Murder has undoubtedly been done, and if Curtis doesn't ride the lightning for it, then who will?

These seven short stories, by well-known writers such as Dashiel Hammett, Patricia Highsmith, and Nancy Pickard, will keep you on the edge of your seat.

Meteor and Other Stories

JOHN WYNDHAM

Retold by Patrick Nobes

It was just a smooth round metal ball, less than a metre in diameter. Although it was still hot from its journey through the huge nothingness of space, it looked quite harmless. But what was it, exactly? A meteor, perhaps – just one of those pieces of rock from outer space that occasionally fall down on to the planet Earth. But meteors don't usually make strange hissing sounds . . .

In this collection of four of his famous science-fiction stories, John Wyndham creates visions of the future that make us think carefully about the way we live now.

Crime Never Pays

Short stories by

AGATHA CHRISTIE, GRAHAM GREENE, DOROTHY L. SAYERS,
SIR ARTHUR CONAN DOYLE, MARGERY ALLINGHAM, RUTH RENDELL,
PATRICIA HIGHSMITH, ANGELA NOEL

Murder: the unlawful, intentional killing of a human being – a terrible crime. But murder stories are always fascinating. Who did it? And how? Or why? Was it murder at all, or just an unfortunate accident? Who will triumph, the murderer or the detective? This collection contains a wide range of murder stories, from the astute detection of the famous Sherlock Holmes, to the chilling psychology of Ruth Rendell.

A Window on the Universe

Short stories by

RAY BRADBURY, BILL BROWN, PHILIP K. DICK,
ARTHUR C. CLARKE, JEROME BIXBY, ISAAC ASIMOV, BRIAN ALDISS,
JOHN WYNDHAM, ROALD DAHL

What does the future hold in store for the human race? Aliens from distant galaxies, telepathic horror, interstellar war, time-warps, the shriek of a rose, collision with an asteroid – the unknown lies around every corner, and the universe is a big place. These nine science-fiction stories offer possibilities that are fantastic, humorous, alarming, but always thought-provoking.